MW01039105

Lincoln's

Better Angel

◆   ◆   ◆

Lincoln's Better Angel

◆   ◆   ◆

DAVID L. SELBY

Mayhaven Publishing, Inc.
P O Box 557
Mahomet, IL 61853
USA

Cover Art and Design by Jack Davis
Copyright © 2007 David L. Selby
First Edition—First Printing 2007
1 2 3 4 5 6 7 8 9 10
Library of Congress Control Number: 2007926716

ISBN-13: 978-193227827-9
ISBN 10: 193227827-3

DEDICATION

This book is dedicated to the ones who gave me courage:
Chippy, Jamison, Brooke, Amanda and Brianna.

I thank David Herbert Donald for his wonderful work and writing
on Lincoln. This work would not have been possible otherwise.
Though I had long admired Lincoln's Gettysburg Address, it was
Gary Wills who made me truly appreciate and understand it.

FOR THE READER

Author and actor, David L. Selby, first wrote this story for the stage. The positive response led him to create this expanded, thought-provoking novel for a broader audience—influenced in substance and style by the play.

—Assistant Editor, Brian Porter

ACKNOWLEDGEMENTS

In the early 1990's, I read an article in the *Washington Post* about James Hudson, a black Vietnam veteran whose job it was to keep the Lincoln Memorial looking beautiful. He died of a heart attack while working his third shift during a scorching July 4 holiday. While this book is not about Mr. Hudson's life, I am thankful for the inspiration that his life gave me, his love for his family, his job, his country, and for Lincoln.

This book would not have been possible if not for the early enthusiasm and encouragement of Bill Lucht and later, the energetic work of Sharla Tandler. Special thanks to Doris Wenzel, my very busy publisher and editor, who was unselfish with her time and insightfulness. Finally, and as always, thanks to my wife Chip who gave her unfailing support along with her constructive, judicious, editing and extensive comments—and all with good humor.

ONE

Charles Huggins rose awkwardly from his bed and drug himself to the bathroom, one painful step at a time. He found it hard to catch a full breath. He splashed cold water on his three-day beard. On the dawn of an already humid, stifling Fourth of July, he leaned his body on the sink and stared into the stained bowl of the vanity. Still wearing his rumpled Park Service uniform, he couldn't recall the last time he had *slept* in his bed. The chair in the living room had become preferable to the cold patch of emptiness left when Darlene had reluctantly given up her side of the bed six months earlier. Charles' hands gripped the sides of the wash basin. His forehead quickly glistened with small pearls of sweat.

Looking into his bathroom mirror, he felt a pang of guilt knowing twenty-five years of never missing a day of work was about to be broken. Despite all the misery, he tried to rally his body, telling himself that he hadn't missed yet. Perhaps, he thought, he could stir himself out of his lethargy. After all, hadn't work kept him sane? He toweled off his face and smoothed the front of his shirt. He had never shied from physical work. He enjoyed it. He had always managed before to lift himself from the depths of gloom — for work.

Charles walked to the apartment window and looked out at the sun's first hazy orange rays over the Shaw District where he and Darlene had lived most of their lives together. In the distance, the sun bathed the Liberty Statue atop Washington D.C.'s Capitol dome. Jefferson Davis, Secretary of War under Franklin Pierce, had been in charge of the remodeling and enlargement of the Capitol during the 1850's. He had disliked the 'liberty cap' that was to adorn the statue's head because it was a symbol for freed slaves, and he had demanded and gotten a change. Then in 1863, when Davis was the President of the Confederacy during the Civil War, the Liberty Statue was put in place with the labor of freed slaves under Lincoln's watch. The irony was not lost on Charles. He turned away from the window and wiped the sweat from the nape of his neck. He felt depleted, found it hard to hold his head erect, his eyes stared — often at nothing.

For fifteen of the twenty-five years he had worked for the National Park Service, Charles' job had been to maintain one of America's most treasured shrines — the Lincoln Memorial. Over time he had felt a certain connection to Lincoln, sometimes actually sharing his joys and his trials outloud, as he worked in the shadow of The Great Emancipator. He had even talked of his recent despair and how he was contemplating taking his own life. He had explained that it was increasingly hard for him to make it from morning to bedtime and back to morning when his daily ritual would begin again. For much of their marriage, Darlene had teased him, "You're like the energizer bunny that just keeps going and going." Those days, he had whispered to the great figure of Lincoln, were over. On this July Fourth morning, his battery had run down.

He looked again out the window and scolded himself: "Come on Charles, you're not the only one suffering. Stop beating your chest."

He shuffled back to the bathroom. The image looking back at him from the mirror revealed a weary man. His wife had told him he was too young for the deep dark circles under his eyes — but she knew they were eyes that told of a terrible, tortured, crushing history and a heart that could find no more inspiration.

On this July Fourth morning, on what would have been their son's twenty-first birthday, a confused, disoriented and deeply saddened Charles held on to the sink, searching his image in the bathroom mirror. In his features, he saw the faces of his son, his father, his brother, and all those who had gone before, blurred together in memory. There in the mirror was everything his ancestors had managed to survive, everything he had survived — until now.

Charles knew why he was suddenly old. He ached with pain from the loss of his son. Now having lost his way, having abandoned what he had struggled for, he just wanted to curl up and die. Charles held out his leathered, calloused hands, fingers spread. They were workingman's hands. He had been proud of that, and he still wore the gold wedding band his wife had bought him before he shipped out to Vietnam. That had been a lifetime ago. They had not been married then, but Darlene didn't want him forgetting the girl back home. Charles rotated the wedding band with his thumb, turned his hands over, palms up, then buried his face in them.

It was several minutes before he ambled into the small, unkempt kitchen. Like the rest of the apartment, it had once been neat and inviting. Now, used food bags, along with a couple of empty cans of beans, were sitting on the counter top next to a set of old Negro-head salt and pepper shakers. There was an empty milk container with a

11

"Have you seen this child?" notice on the side panel. He could not avert his eyes fast enough. The chaos was so unlike Charles. He liked everything in its place. If the morning paper was in disarray or a picture crooked on the wall, he had to remedy it. Even now the urge to put things in their place drifted across his mind.

Charles walked into the living room and opened a closet door. He reached his hand back in the furthest corner. From under some old marine discharge papers and tax receipts, he pulled out a Glock gun and a box of ammo that he had shamefully bought when he and Darlene moved with young son Richie into an area filled with young black men. He felt he had let the negative reputations of black men, men like him, become a reality. Charles carried the gun to the window and laid it on the sill. The street was empty. The middle-class Shaw District would soon start coming to life.

Charles stared. There was a Harlequin-dressed figure pushing a grocery cart down the middle of the still quiet street. Charles recognized the man, a musician. For the last several months, he could be seen most days playing his sax at the Lincoln Memorial. Charles rubbed his glistening forehead, soaked with sweat, with his sleeve. He loaded bullets into the magazine of the 9mm semiautomatic pistol. He was not afraid to die, but still he looked around. He should straighten the place up a bit first. "Always ready for company," Darlene had always joked.

The glare of the sun poured through the window, as though determined to scour away the sadness that permeated the room and seeped into the walls. Charles turned back to the living room. Several collections of Shakespeare, an open Bible, some African-American art, a photo of Martin Luther King, several books with Lincoln in the title, and a photo of the statue of Lincoln with Charles irreverently seated in his lap lined the bookshelves.

A table was covered with photos, including one of Charles and his brother Terry with some friends in front of the Lincoln Memorial during Reverend King's famous *I Have A Dream* speech. There was a photo of Charles and Darlene with Richie at his high school graduation. Almost hidden behind other photos were pictures of Charles from Vietnam with his sunglasses-adorned buddy "Willie from Philly" and a photo of Charles as a young marine in dress uniform with Darlene, his bride to be. There was a memorial of photos of his son in childhood, in teenage years, and of him as a proud smiling young man in his Marine dress uniform. Charles wanted the photos to fool him into believing Richie was still alive.

Charles glanced toward a closed door leading off the living room — Richie's room. Charles had not entered it since the day two Marines knocked on their apartment door and informed them of Richie's death. Charles had objected to giving away any of his son's clothes or personal items as though he expected his son to return. He had often found himself asking his dead son questions or telling him some bit of information he thought would be of interest.

Charles put his hand on the doorknob but did not turn the handle. Let it go, he thought. He knew what was on the other side. His son's computer would be dormant. Files of his family history research would still be on the computer's desktop, and beside the bed a few unopened boxes of his son's belongings sent back from Iraq.

Charles walked past the sun-drenched window to the linen closet where he got a towel. He carefully placed it over the back of a chair and sat down. He didn't want to make a mess, and for some crazy reason, he mused, he didn't want to shoot himself standing up because he would fall to the floor. Better to be seated, he thought, staring at the ceiling. The clock read 6:32 AM. He closed his eyes. His mind went blank. Then an image of himself as a young boy, face pressed against an unpainted, worn screen door, looking out on a field of white cotton appeared. When he opened his eyes, he noticed that the clock read 7:12 AM.

Except for that fleeting image, it seemed to Charles that he and his family had been annihilated. It seemed, too, there were no longer any options for him. He did not blame his wife for moving out. She had gone reluctantly when he told her of his need to be alone. When she was safely out of the house, he made sure his personal effects were in order. He would have been better off, he darkly thought, if his ancestors had taken Lincoln up on his offer to send them to Liberia. "Liberia!" had been Charles' reaction when Richie told him what Lincoln had entertained for the newly freed slaves.

Without further deliberation Charles leaned his forehead into the muzzle of the gun. He was oblivious to the sound of cars and people on the street. His eyes were closed. He breathed deeply once, then held his breath. His finger pulsed.

At that second, the alarm on the clock beside his bed blared. Charles' hand flinched and the gun swung upward, the barrel hitting his lip.

"Bless it!"

He shook his head, his lip was smarting from the small cut. The alarm blaring, he got up, walked into the bedroom and turned it off. Touching his bloody lip he glanced at the mirror over his dresser.

"You'll live," he said.

He walked back to the chair and to the gun. The phone rang. He looked at the phone but didn't move. The phone rang again and again. For a second he considered answering it, but let it go. The answering machine picked up. Darlene's taped greeting was on the machine: "We're not here, but leave us a message and we will do our absolute best to see you get called back."

The same assured voice came onto the line. Charles looked at her photo on the table.

"Hey. It's me. Are you there? What a day. It's strange, you know. It's been two years since . . . . Well, I just wanted to say . . . are you eating? I thought I'd get you before you went to work. Give me a call . . . if you want. You know where I am."

He stared at the phone and then toward the gun still in his hand. The sound of a siren outside the window brought him closer to reality. He glanced at the clock. 7:45 A.M. He placed the gun on the table beside his chair and retreated to the bathroom. He threw some more cold water over his face and looked at his unshaven image.

"Growing a beard, Charles?" he said to his reflection.

He knew someone would ask about his lip. He dried his face, and picked up his keys from the hall table, glancing at Lincoln's picture.

TWO

Charles stepped out onto the front stoop of his five-story apartment building. The small lawn, divided by an uneven cement walkway, was in need of cutting. He noticed the large flowerpot sitting just outside the front door. There was a small wooden cross, painted white, in the middle of the pot and surrounded with a well-tended cluster of blooming flowers, a memorial gift from his fellow apartment dwellers. Charles had tried to ignore it, but the plants looked thirsty. He brought a hose from around the side of the building and gave them a needed drink.

His mind drifted to Darlene's message. Two years ago Marines in dress uniform had walked up that sidewalk. Darlene had opened the door. Oh yes, he remembered:

◆　◆　◆

"Mrs. Huggins?"

"Yes," Darlene answered hesitantly, fearful of what was coming.

"We regret to inform you that your son has been killed in action," said the stoic Marine. Darlene didn't hear another word.

It took a long moment for her to grasp what she had been told. Then she cried out for Charles. When he got to her side, she fell into his arms. The Marines quietly excused themselves saying their son's personal items would soon arrive. When the door shut, Charles fell to his knees, holding onto a sobbing Darlene. He erupted with a deep primal cry in uncontrollable anguish. Yes, he remembered.

◆　◆　◆

Charles pulled himself up into his old Ford Bronco. Driving down the block, he was sure he saw the same two marines that had come to his door that fateful morning. Charles slowed the Bronco and watched the Marines walk purposely up to a house. "They're not bringing good news," he said to himself as he speeded up, unable to avoid the unspeakable pain in the pit of his stomach. Too many families would be starting the day the same sorrowful way — the same as families from other wars, for all wars — when the "angels of death" come calling.

He nearly ran a red light. A group of kids were standing at the corner waiting for a bus. He had counseled his son not to stand too long at a bus stop, fearful of a drive-by shooter. Most days Charles had made Richie come straight home from school. He hadn't allowed him to play in the street. He encouraged his son to invite his friends home where they could play indoors. Richie had sometimes made fun of his father's caution about dangers in D.C.

"It's a safe town," he would tell his dad. "The chance of something happening to me in D.C. is like a train wreck."

"I see train wrecks every day in D.C."

"I never ride the train," Richie would counter, laughing. He had made the mistake of telling his dad about an escapade at school where gunshots rang out. Charles knew it was proof life was more dangerous for Richie than it had been for him as a child.

"If you hear gunshots, fall to the floor. And don't get up when the shooting stops because they're just reloading."

When he learned Richie was going to Iraq, he tried to ask his son questions that would make him think about what he was about to do. Charles knew well the feeling of waking with his face in mud and blood.

"Am I going to live?"

"I think so," the young medic had replied. All these years later, Charles now wished that medic had been wrong.

A horn blared behind him.

"Sorry," he waved.

◆   ◆   ◆

Charles was taking his habitual route to work. It was the long way around, but it gave him a chance to check on many of the nation's memorials. The Shaw District, near lower-income, higher crime areas, had modest largely well-kept houses and apartment buildings. The District was named after the white leader, Col. Robert Gould Shaw of the first African-American regiment—the Fifty-Fourth Massachusetts—formed in 1863. Col. Shaw was shot through the heart in the battle on Fort Wagner outside Charleston, South Carolina, in July of 1863, his body dumped in a ditch by the enemy. Charles had wanted Richie to know about the "black regiment" and about the valiant and true man who had led them. He had taken his wife and son on a train trip to Boston where they saw the Civil War monument in Boston Common.

◆　◆　◆

"A tremendous death toll was taken, but the black soldiers never wavered."

"Yes, I know, Dad," Richie had replied, reminding his father that he had seen the movie *Glory*.

The highlight of the trip for Richie was getting to take in a Boston Red Sox baseball game at Fenway Park. He had made a wager with his dad that the Sox would win the World Series that year. Charles figured he had a sure thing — the Sox would fold. Charles lost, but it was worth it, as they saw Shaw's monument.

Returning home, he had quizzed his son:

"Who was the artist of the sculpture?"

"What was it in tribute to?"

"Who was Col. Shaw?"

"Was he white?"

"Why was he a hero?"

Richie had mildly complained about this quiz game, but his father reminded him, "It's not baseball, not just a game. It keeps your mind sharp. It's good for your powers of observation and helps you to understand how a person's actions may transcend whatever cause they're fighting for."

◆　◆　◆

On this July Fourth morning, Charles noticed that the new visitors center being built at the Capitol was near completion. Cement barriers were in place, erected everywhere around the capital.

"You're nobody if you don't have a barrier," Charles had told Darlene months earlier.

Ever since 2001, jackhammers and backhoes ruled the day in D.C. Walls, chain-link fences, checkpoints, massive concrete planters and steel posts, metal detectors, surveillance cameras, along with flak-jacketed police officers, spread out all over the capital.

"A fortress," he rued to Darlene.

Charles often held court at the family's dinner hour about how the people already felt removed from the political game because of special interests and lobbyists.

"Now when they see all those barriers, that will be the end of free and open government as far as they're concerned. You make the monuments too difficult for people to see, the terrorists win."

His head was pounding. Sweat dripped. It was going to be a sweltering day for the nation's birthday. The National Weather Service had already put out a heat advisory warning residents to slow down, wear light-colored clothes and drink plenty of water.

Traffic was still light though, and Charles easily made his way down Pennsylvania Avenue along the Mall. Several black limos were already waiting at the gate of the White House while the drivers spoke with uniformed marines. On the Mall surrounding the Washington Monument, the Stars and Stripes were being raised while workers were already busy making preparations to celebrate America's birthday. Washington's Monument was newly landscaped with security barriers. Charles had to admit that they had done a pretty good job.

There would be the usual fireworks and patriotic music along with a speech or two, July Fourth being the embodiment of the heart and soul of the United States. Despite a raised security alert, promise was in the air as the United States was set to celebrate another birthday with one of the biggest bashes ever held in the nation's Capital.

◆ ◆ ◆

"You know some people once wanted to move the capital," Richie had told his dad during one of their nightly sessions as to what had transpired during Richie's school day.

"In the early 1800's, there was talk of moving the capital out west, toward the center of the country. Congress, though, decided to keep Washington as the capital."

"That's one decision they got right," said Charles.

"Conditions were improved, new public buildings were built. So that ended any talk of moving the capital," Richie had informed his father.

Charles eventually found himself in front of the Jefferson Memorial. He slowed down and surveyed the scene, lamenting the security barricades that made it especially hard for older people to fully enjoy the Memorial. Red, white, and blue banners already flew, but most were in a pile waiting to be hung. A few National Parks employees stood around trying to deny the beginning of what, for most of them, would be the hardest workday of the year.

"Hey, Charles," a couple of them called out.

Charles stared at them. They snapped to and started to work without saying anything else.

He edged his car into a parking spot and took the key out of the ignition. He sat there, unable to move. There were several police mulling about. A noisy helicopter flew low, a nod to the orange terror alert, which he, like most others, ignored.

The Lincoln Memorial with its rich stacks of Georgian marble loomed in the distance like a Greek temple. When Charles began to work at the Lincoln Memorial, its grandeur had made it practically impossible for him to think of Lincoln as anything but a god. The words chiseled into the walls of the Memorial defined, he thought, what America was about. Charles had never questioned those words.

Dedicated in 1922, the Memorial sits in Potomac Park just beyond the newest memorial, dedicated to the men and women who fought in WW II. There had been talk that there was no more room on the Mall for another museum or monument, but another report concluded that there was plenty of room for at least fifty more monuments. There was, as usual Charles thought, no mention of a museum dedicated to slavery. This had always perplexed him.

◆ ◆ ◆

"Why do people continue to deny that slavery and race are the centerpieces of American history?"

Darlene had looked up from the comic section of the morning paper. Charles didn't expect an answer. She always started the morning with the comics. Charles took the front page section. They had shared some good laughs thinking that Jefferson Davis, the president of the South and an opponent of Lincoln's, would be turning over in his grave if he knew that marble from the old confederate state of Georgia had supplied the marble for Lincoln's statue. Being from Georgia, it pleased Charles.

Every morning when he walked up the Memorial steps, he read the words to Reverend King's *I Have a Dream* speech which had recently been etched into them. He could hear King's distant voice in his head speaking with his familiar tone, "I have a dream . . ."

Charles had been there in July of 1963 listening, mesmerized by the great preacher. Only a few years prior, Rosa Parks had refused to give up her bus seat to a white man.

"Rosa Parks is a brave woman," Charles' mother had told him. "One person *can* make a big difference."

That's what Richie had said. "I can make a difference, Dad. Maybe I'll run for office."

Their mother had taken Charles and his brother Terry to hear Dr. King that day. She took a photo of the two boys, and Charles had found it in her Bible after she died. He'd framed it and set it on a shelf in his house.

Charles had only gone back to his home state of Georgia once after he grew up — to find his father's grave. He knew that in Georgia blacks and whites worked and ate together, went to school together, perhaps more than they do in the north. Back in Lincoln's day, he mused, blacks weren't allowed in some northern states. In Lincoln's home state of Illinois, blacks had to pay a $1,000 bond to enter the state. These were more things Charles had learned from his son's research on the internet for his school papers.

"Back in Lincoln's time," Richie said, "we wouldn't have been able to spend the night in some states. And you wouldn't have had to serve on that jury because we weren't allowed to be on juries. Also, you wouldn't have had to go to Vietnam because you couldn't have been in the military."

"I wanted to go to Vietnam," Charles said, then quickly changed the conversation. He had delighted in the give and take with his son. America had come a long way in racial relations in the last 50 years, he told Richie, "but it was too late for your grandfather."

Charles had tried mightily to convince himself that racism no longer affected his life or his son's life, although many of Charles' friends, and his son's friends, thought racism was still a big problem. Charles wondered about his own inferiority. Did he inherit this from his daddy, and his daddy from his daddy? Did he unknowingly pass it down to his son? Charles had let that notion slide. He felt blacks had bigger problems.

◆ ◆ ◆

Charles finally willed himself out of the Bronco, stumbling a moment, and made his way toward the Memorial. He was definitely not pleased with the plans to build a wall around it and had complained to his superiors, but it was out of their hands.

"It's bigger than us," they chimed.

"Lincoln's a man of the people; the Memorial should remain a people's memorial," he urged.

Red, white, and blue signs were abundant. One fellow was already parading as Uncle Sam.

A fellow worker passed by. "Hello, Charles."

Charles gave a nod and a slight murmur of response not meant to be heard. The soulful tones of a saxophone wafted through the air as they had for several months. For these soothing sounds, Charles was most grateful. He stopped and listened. The Musician's music had sustained and diverted Charles' spirits during his grim struggle. He thought the Musician was the Miles Davis of the saxophone. He was sparse in his playing. It was fitting, Charles thought, that the Musician had set up shop at the base of the Lincoln Memorial. Both the Musician and Lincoln had a kind of poetic quality. The Musician's haunting music seemed appropriate on this birthday morning.

A grocery cart, decorated with colored ribbons, a horn and bell ringer attached to the handle, sat off to the side of the Musician. The cart was full of the Musician's belongings, a magical grab bag of chaos and color. He was dressed, as he had been earlier in the morning when he walked by Charles' apartment window, like a patchwork-quilt-Harlequin from Winslow Homer's painting. Charles had seen the painting, *The Carnival,* at the National Gallery with Darlene and Richie.

◆ ◆ ◆

"The Harlequin's coat of many colors," they overheard a tourist — probably a teacher — saying, "signifies that his 'self' is not confined within a single color." They had gotten a kick out of that.

◆ ◆ ◆

When they could, Charles and Darlene had loved to take in a local club featuring live jazz. Now he watched the Musician playing his saxophone and walked toward him. As usual the Musician's eyes were adorned with sunglasses. A few people were listening to his music. They were among those already camped out on the steps of the Lincoln Memorial, staking out their seats for the evening's festivities. They tossed a few coins into the Musician's red and blue Dr. Seuss-like hat. The Musician smiled and nodded to them as he played. He finished his tune.

Charles stepped toward him. "What are you doing here, man? Whole town's going to be up the way celebrating."

He knew the man was a fine musician and hated to see him performing for people who would probably not appreciate him. There were better places to be. "Wanna see any folding stuff, not just pocket change, you better move your store. Lightning ain't gonna hit here — too hot for lightning."

The musician nodded giving a deep bow with dramatic flourish. Then he set his sax in his cart and rolled it off, disappearing into the crowd. Charles watched him go. For a second, the slightest of smiles flickered across his face, a smile his wife had always said, "could melt ice cubes."

The Fourth of July had always been a busy time for Charles

because of the 250,000 tourists who left behind food wrappers, soda cans, and all sorts of trash. In fact, he almost always worked two shifts and never complained. He just hoped the litterbugs took something positive away from their visits. Charles was walking toward the figure of Lincoln when a loud firecracker went off. Charles flinched, but kept moving.

"They're already starting," he complained to himself.

The Lincoln Memorial had been more than a job. Charles considered it his personal responsibility, a responsibility for the care and cleaning of the marble figure of Lincoln. He gave it a daily dusting and a frequent wash down.

Charles never seemed to be too concerned with the heat of summer or the dead cold of winter when taking care of his beloved Lincoln Memorial. Heat and cold were just a part of it — first as a laborer, then as foreman of the maintenance crew who looked after America's shrines. It was an important job, though for many years the Memorial had no full time workers because of tight budgets. Charles was diligent and dedicated and had never complained about his salary, which allowed few luxuries for his family. Many of the extras came from his wife's salary as an elementary school teacher. Still, he was content to make an honest living. He never went through the motions. He epitomized the struggling blue-collar, laboring man who had endured every form of adversity over the years and still took pride in his work. This was the kind of man, Charles thought, Lincoln had talked about with admiration.

Charles had requested the Memorial job after a friend and fellow Vietnam veteran had died of a heat stroke after working a double shift at the Lincoln Memorial on July Fourth, 1992. Ironically, and sadly, it was because of his friend's death that Charles and others working for the National Park Service had been elevated to full-time status and given full medical coverage. His friend's death had caused an uproar in Washington when it was disclosed that many Park Service employees were kept on a part-time basis so they would not have to be paid benefits. Because his friend's family could not afford funeral services, the outrage was such that the law was changed. Charles had told Darlene that there should be a statue to his friend on the Mall.

Some time afterwards, Charles requested the Lincoln Memorial assignment. He vowed to honor his friend with his work.

◆　◆　◆

Charles thought about that as he started to climb the Memorial steps, looking from side to side and up and down. He never missed anything that needed grooming at the Memorial and would laughingly tell his family how much dirt there was behind Lincoln's ears. He knew how carbon monoxide from cars, mixed with other impurities in the air, settled on the marble causing deterioration. He could see it just as he could see the red dust acid rain left on the tomato plants he used to tend in a vacant lot near his apartment.

He looked up at Lincoln. Ordinarily he would greet the President. "Good morning. Hot day. I don't mind heat or cold, no sir. Got to keep scratching, I know because the car needs work, apartment needs painting. Work, work, work is the main thing. Haven't I heard that enough. And in this job, if you don't, it don't matter anyway because they're afraid to fire your butt." And Charles would laugh, sure that Lincoln enjoyed the humor.

This day, however, he continued quietly up the stairs toward the imposing statue. It sat some 19 feet high. Charles looked around. He knew by early evening the Memorial steps would be packed full of spectators for the July 4th fireworks. He looked again into the face of President Lincoln and thought, Mr. President, you may be weathered and worried, but you have the best seat to see out across the Mall. The somber eyes seemed to be pondering some great question no one else was privy to. The shoulders seemed to carry an unseen weight across their wide expanse, but there was a steadfast determination in his posture. Considering the state of the world, Charles knew someone in the growing crowd was wondering how Lincoln would handle the problems at hand.

He slapped the statue as he passed by and shook his head thinking that he spied another bird's nest resting on Lincoln's shoulder. It had appeared overnight. He was always removing bird nests from Lincoln's statue. Birds were attracted by spiders, who were attracted by midges, who were attracted by the spotlights that lit up the Memorial at night — another endless battle that Charles was losing. He had finally convinced his superiors to delay turning on the lights for a period of time because the daily scrubbing was not good for the Georgian marble. He was pleased when the Park Service bought him a new machine that sucked up the water from the floor allowing it to dry much faster.

He had delighted in telling Darlene and Richie tales about his adventures on the job, including the time he fell off his ladder into Lincoln's lap, something a tourist had captured on film and given to him. Another picture of him standing on Lincoln's shoulder cleaning out the statue's ears had made the front page of *The Washington Post*. Darlene had it framed and hung it in their living room.

Charles had been fond of taking his wife and son on special tours of the memorial tributes, especially at sunset. He loved the way the shadows slid across the monuments. He had even taken them on a short cruise down the Potomac River at sunset so they could see the sun's golden hue cast on the Lincoln Memorial. He truly thought D.C. was the most beautiful city he had seen, and despite everything, he had loved being able to live there. He was pleased to be able to call D.C. home. And the Shaw District was a place he and Darlene had chosen to live. Charles knew, for many blacks, there was no choice. He had been ever thankful to his share-cropper father who had moved the family north in search of a better life. Charles had always been honored to work at the Lincoln Memorial. He paused below the memorial. All that seemed a long time ago.

THREE

Charles was high on the ladder dressed in a yellow slicker holding a scrub-hose giving Lincoln a bath. Charles wiped the beads of
perspiration from his forehead with a rag.

"This ladder gets longer every day," he said aloud to no one.

He reached over with the rag and cleaned a smudge off the nose
of the statue. He then brushed hard on a spot on the statue's forehead.

Just then a helicopter skimmed the Potomac and banked low
right over top of the Memorial. Charles held still until it was gone.

He shot the statue's face a round of water. Then he began to ease
his way down the ladder.

"Your hands are filthy. That's an impressive achievement for a
man who doesn't move around."

It was then that something in Lincoln's lap caught his eye.

"Jesus."

It was a rope noose with a note attached. He glanced at the note.

An audible moan escaped from his lips. He looked up at Lincoln wondering just what *was* behind those soulful eyes, and for the first time in days, he spoke to Mr. Lincoln.

"What do you see out there? What do you know?"

"Who did this?" He held the noose up for Lincoln to see.

Charles climbed down the ladder, missing the last rung and falling onto the floor. He pulled himself up and made his way into the small gift shop that sold books and touristy items. He poured himself a cup of watered down coffee and found an aspirin bottle behind the counter. He washed three down with a single sip.

Alice Johnson was a middle-aged no-nonsense woman busily organizing and getting the store ready to open. She was one of the first National Park employees Charles had met when he had started working for the Park Service. He liked her instantly because she pretty much said what was on her mind. He was at a loss though, as to why the coffee was never better, but he never complained. He raised his cup to her in salute. Her smile was tentative. He sensed she was about to go into her morning analysis of him. She, like other workers, was well intentioned. She was dismayed by what was happening to her friend.

He had tried hard at first to keep up appearances — a face for all occasions. Soon Charles grew tired of people asking if he was all right and tired of pretending to be. He understood they wanted to help. He knew there was no help that would take away the painful loss and attending, grinding grief.

◆ ◆ ◆

"Compensation," Charles, had muttered distastefully when told by a government official that because of their son's death, he and

Darlene were entitled to some monetary award. Charles could barely contain himself. He could not, would not discuss "compensation." It was not possible. Charles had struggled mightily with depression when he came home from Vietnam, and since his son had been killed, he had shut himself off from everyone including his wife. He could only howl at the wind, a madman, until there was no more breath, until there was no one to hear him, no one to offer a hand that he would refuse.

That first autumn after Richie's death, Charles had come down with a bad cold, another in a series of ailments. Darlene was worried not just about her husband's physical health, but his mental health as well. She told him he needed help. "This is not something that's going to go away. Time is not going to heal this wound."

They could both go to the doctor, she had told him. She pleaded daily with him to go. "We can make it through this, Charles."

He had refused. He had trouble sleeping. He lost so much weight he wasn't always recognized by others.

"Depression and stress are the only diet plans that ever worked for me," he joked. He started drinking.

Darlene tried anger. "You have an obligation to go on."

After a year and a half, he told her to go. She didn't want to, but she was unable to find a way for them to continue on together. If he would not seek help, she would have to leave him. She prayed that her leaving would propel him to do something to save himself. She moved in with her ailing mother.

Though he didn't want to see anybody, Charles had insisted on working. People gave him room. They avoided him when possible. He was not good company anymore. He didn't have the energy. He was surly and agitated, short-tempered and indifferent to daily events. His fellow workers could not bring him out of his shell of emptiness. He had reason for his overwhelming sadness and began to resent any intrusions, well meaning or not.

The people who wanted to help him were friends, people who cared for him. They would call and remind him to eat. He was embarrassed. He didn't want sympathy. Didn't need it, he said. There was nothing anyone could do. He asked them to ignore him. "I don't exist."

Alice Johnson ignored his request to ignore him. "You growing those whiskers for my benefit or you just trying to emulate your friend?" She got no response.

"You ready for the party?"

Still no response.

"You don't look good."

"I feel worse than I look."

Alice looked up. She was surprised to get an answer. It had been months since she had heard him say anything. She played it cool.

"That's why they have sick days. Your friend wouldn't miss you for a day.

"I sure wouldn't miss this coffee," Charles said, taking another sip.

"You pass Starbucks every morning."

The repartee between the two friends picked up where it had left off. He tossed the noose on the counter.

"No thank you." After the moment she took to collect herself she asked, "Where'd you find this?"

"President's lap."

"Mercy, mercy. How'd it get there?"

Charles shrugged and started to leave.

"What am I supposed to do with it?"

"Sell it," he said. "Strange fruit, America's pastime."

Charles' father had told him about a lynching of a white man that he had witnessed in Georgia. "Must have been a bad dude. It was a social event."

"Anti-lynching," said Charles sarcastically to Alice, "was the last major civil rights issue the Republicans were out in front on."

"Don't I know it," she said.

Charles had tried to act nonchalant about the noose, but he was bothered. Alice, however, was riled.

"This is unspeakable. We can't let it slide."

Charles didn't respond.

"We won't let it slide, will we?"

Besides her genuine anger, there was the hope that Charles would get his back up, that it would be a diversion for him. This could be just the medicine he needed, she thought. Charles started once again to leave.

"Charles?"

He shook his head and mumbled something about work to do.

"What's more important than this?" She got right in front of him holding the noose in his face. She didn't seem to understand the meaning of "no."

"Not today," he said, trying to brush past her. He didn't want to deal with it. He couldn't. This was too much for him at the moment. He'd seen other racist things left at Lincoln's statue.

Alice countered his retreat. "I was just reading," she said, "about a couple of redneck prosecutors walking into a courtroom with bright red ties . . ." Charles started to interrupt her to say he'd read the article, but he realized she would not be deterred. ". . . with six-inch white nooses on them that were knitted by one of their wives. That woman took a lot of time and care to knit those nooses. Can you imagine? I'd like to knit her a noose!"

The writing on the note, "Nigger lover," caught her eye.

"Lord Almighty. Did you see this?"

Charles nodded.

"We have to complain."

"You do that."

"Charles, are you ok?"

"Yeah, Alice, I'm fine."

"What are we going to do?" She was still blocking his path.

"Please."

"Who would do this?"

". . . Kids."

"Doesn't matter. It's racist. Right?"

"Who else got strung up."

"So, we have to speak up about things like this."

"Don't make me step on your toes," said Charles trying to get by her.

"Charles!"

"Call Homeland Security."

"We can't let it go. Can't just sweep it under the rug."

He shook his head and was out the door dumping the tasteless coffee in the trash on the way.

"It's the Fourth of July," she called out to him.

FOUR

Charles, away from Alice's voice, was more depressed than he thought possible. He was angry about the noose. Alice was right on that, and for that brief moment he hadn't thought about himself and his pain. For that brief moment he wanted to do something besides die, but what good would complaining do? Years ago, he would have lost his job, but this was a different time. He wouldn't lose his job, but it could get ugly. He knew his brother Terry would have done something. Willie, his Vietnam buddy, would have staged a scene of epic proportions. Charles wanted to hit something, throw something. He wanted to cry but couldn't. There were no more tears.

He fell against the wall with the Gettysburg Address engraved over his head. He needed to get away, to put the noose out of his sight. He knew what a stir it would cause. He had just heard a news item about a white supremacy group holding a meeting in North or South Carolina. He knew you couldn't ignore something like this even if it was just a prank. Malcolm nor Martin would have let it go. How could it be, he thought. Had he just been a fence sitter all these years? Was "Willie from Philly" right when he said, "Huggins, you're not black enough." Had his older brother done the better thing by avoiding Vietnam and fighting racial injustice here at home?

Charles spent years after the Vietnam war, after King's death, after all the protests, after too many complaints and committees, minding his own business, going home to his wife and son. It had been another lifetime. Nothing could make a difference. Nothing. Not even the hideous reminder of what a piece of rope meant. Wasn't it just the other morning he read that the KKK was going to demonstrate at the Gettysburg Cemetery over the Fourth?

He walked around the Memorial to the other side of the statue where he caught his breath remembering his mother's advice, "Keep to the rhythm and you won't get lost." His hands were wet with sweat. He walked quick circles around the statue—once, twice. He stood breathing heavily at the top of the steps just behind a velvet rope stretched across the top of the Memorial stairs. He looked down the steps and across the Mall. People were beginning to congregate. Police worked along side the Parks Service workers getting the place ready for the celebration of music, speeches and fireworks. Serious-faced, flak jacketed, armed soldiers were keeping watch. Charles looked at his watch, took a deep breath, trying desperately to look normal. When his watch read 9:00 AM, he called: "Open him up."

He watched the young worker unclip the rope and roll it up. A large gaggle of school children led by a few flustered adults headed up the stairs. The children, having been held back by teachers trying to maintain some semblance of order, were running to see who would reach the top first.

"And they're off," Charles said flatly.

The children surged past Charles on both sides. A boy dropped his candy wrapper on the floor only to meet Charles' pointed iron glare. The boy quickly picked up the wrapper and stuffed it in his pocket and hurried to the other side of the Memorial.

The boy was no more or less disrespectful than some other Fourth of July visitors. It had been Charles' experience that most people, on most days, are affected by their visit to the Memorial. Most are usually very quiet as they look at Lincoln and read the words of the Gettysburg Address and the Second Inaugural. It seemed for them, as it had always been for Charles, an emotional experience.

Charles gathered himself, breaking free of the maze of children. He walked among the people using a broom and dustbin to collect the trash the tourists shed like a second skin. Hundreds of people surged in and out and around the Memorial. They were varying nationalities including, Charles noticed, a couple of adult Arabs in traditional dress with two young girls, their covered heads drawing more than a few stares.

Charles moved along the wall, his back pressed against the chiseled words of Lincoln's Second Inaugural speech. People were endlessly asking him to take pictures of them with the statue.

"No."

"Could you smile," they would ask.

"No."

Words jumped out from the tourists catching his ear as he passed among them watching them stare up at Lincoln.

"So graceful."

"Strong."

"The Great Emancipator."

"I think he looks tender."

"That's a handsome man."

"Sexy."

"Look at those big ears and nose."

"Look at those hands. Big feet."

"How'd they make that?"

"He won the Civil War and freed the slaves."

"Started the income tax."

"He's the daddy of big government."

Charles watched the tourists, considering their words. He saw one student mouthing the Gettysburg Address.

"Now we are engaged in a great civil war . . ."

"Say 'em out loud," Charles encouraged. "Those words are meant for the ear. You want to hear them."

"I don't. I don't like poetry," said the student and walked off. A teacher smiled at Charles.

"Wonderful words," she said and then added just a bit self-consciously. "The price of freedom." The teacher smiled again and went to catch up with her students.

Charles watched her go. He then turned back to the Gettysburg Address and said to himself, thinking about the noose and what it stood for — and about his son, "The price of freedom."

Charles crossed out onto the steps of the Memorial and sat down for a moment. He had started feeling faint. Maybe the student had a point. Suddenly, in the din about him, he spoke: "Poetry. Maybe that's why no one hears your words Mr. President. People don't see what they're seeing, don't hear what they're hearing." He looked back toward Lincoln.

Students stumbled through memorizing those words in school — and then they were forgotten. Charles agreed with the teacher.

He thought the words were the best he had ever heard about the price of freedom. But as Darlene would remind him, the promises were long overdue. They needed to be redeemed.

"Perseverance," Darlene said, "What good is it?" She had said this to Charles after he had expressed his anger about what had happened or wasn't happening in New Orleans.

FIVE

Mid-afternoon and the Mall spread out before Charles and Lincoln through the center of the capital like a green carpet speckled with the blue of the reflecting pond and the white stone of the formal buildings. People milled about in ever-growing numbers — spectators and workers—all preparing for the celebration. The selling and buying of America's birthday had always been a little perplexing for Charles, but he guessed that's what the people wanted.

Across the way the Musician was back, lounging in a ratty old beach chair beside his cart. A cardboard sign hung off the cart reading, "Get Rich Now. Ask Me How!"

The Musician's face was aglow from the mid-morning sun. Despite the heat, he looked peaceful, reassuring as he waved and smiled up at Charles leaning on his broom. Charles returned a slight grin. The musician arose and walked over to his grocery cart of belongings. That's all that man has, Charles thought as the Musician picked up his sax and commenced to play, but maybe that's enough.

He noticed a woman, late forties, coming smartly and quickly up the Memorial stairs in a two-piece red suit with a U.S. flag pin on her lapel. She was followed by a large entourage hurrying to keep up. A politician. Charles recognizing her as an ardent combatant of the president. Seeing the people scurrying around her was a far cry from Lincoln's day, he mused.

"You won the Civil War with three clerks on your staff."

Charles had seen many politicians pay a visit to President Lincoln, rub shoulders with him. Lincoln it seemed appealed to all politicians no matter what party. When the woman and her followers reached the statue, a photographer said, "Give us a smile, Senator." The senator flashed her charismatic smile and made a short speech to a few reporters.

These photo gatherings had become a headache for Charles because they interfered with the tourists. The Memorial had become sort of a national soapbox for any and all causes. The Senator's aides leaned against the statue while listening to their boss. Charles softly cleared his throat, gave the aides the evil eye, motioning for them to get their paws off the statue. Two aides stood up straight as they caught the look in Charles' eyes, and quickly moved away as though they thought he would turn them in to the "race" police.

"I got 250,000 people passing through here today and if they all put their paws on the statue, it'll topple over," he mumbled to a group of tourists watching the senator, only a few of whom know who she was. Charles was notorious to many in the Park Service. He considered the Memorial his domain. It was a wonder, they joked, that he didn't make people remove their shoes before entering. Charles thought it would be a good idea. His mother had made him and his brother always take off their shoes and leave them outside the door of their home.

◆　◆　◆

The picture session over. The Senator and her entourage headed down the stairs with one of the aide's doing his best Lincoln impersonation, "Four score and seven years ago, our fathers brought forth on this. . . ." Suddenly the aide stopped, evidently forgetting what came next.

Charles could not resist and called out, " 'Continent! A new nation, conceived in Liberty and dedicated to the proposition that all men are created equal!' "

Everyone in the senator's party turned back to look up the stairs as Charles was speaking. The tourists were laughing.

"Thank you," called the embarrassed aide to Charles. Another aide broke out laughing and slapped his fellow aide on the back.

Charles knew the aide hadn't heard what he had been quoting. The senator's aides could still be heard laughing as they reached the bottom of the stairs. Perhaps they were laughing, Charles thought, because they knew what his son, Richie had said . . . .

"The 'fathers,' Dad, that Lincoln referred to in the first line of his Gettysburg speech, didn't bring freedom to the slaves and not to the Indians, either."

Charles argued that it was a little more complicated.

"The *fathers*, like Washington and Jefferson, owned large numbers of slaves themselves," his son added. "So how really dedicated were they to the 'proposition that all men are created equal?' "

Charles conceded that his son had a point.

◆　◆　◆

No wonder the senator's aides were having such a good laugh, Charles told the tourists. "Look at 'em, slapping each other on the back, telling each other how much alike we all are — like a broken record." The tourists chuckled.

Charles was quite the entertainer, like an actor who despite feeling blue still gives the audience a show. Charles' audience was an appreciative one.

"They all come to the temple when it suits them, politicians on pilgrimage, their trip to Mecca, praying for redemption. A little catechism, especially when they're campaigning. They like to lay their hands on the throne. They all feel safe associating with Lincoln. No mistresses, no drugs, no voting fraud associated with him. Politicians today want some of Lincoln's compassion to rub off on 'em."

◆　◆　◆

"Lincoln's words sounded good," Charles remembered his son saying.

Was Lincoln doing a little whitewashing or was he trying to redefine the 'founders' words? Was Lincoln trying to make those words mean something the founding fathers didn't mean? These had been perplexing questions for Charles. They were still just as perplexing. He knew Lincoln was a plain spoken, regular guy. Charles had explained this to his son, "Lincoln upheld the notion of politics as an honorable profession. He listened to both sides. He knew when to compromise and when to dig in his heels."

Motivated by his son, Charles had thought a lot about Lincoln's words. He had read them over and over on the south wall of the Memorial under the mural depicting the Emancipation with the

Angel of Truth freeing a slave. He had been reading those words a lot of years. He had taken those words to heart, believed them with every fiber of his body. But what was Lincoln really saying with those words?

Charles had to memorize the Gettysburg Address in high school. He had pasted a copy of the Address into a scrapbook when he was in the ninth grade. He had showed that scrapbook to his son.

"You been snowballed, Dad," his son would tease.

Had this snowball simply gotten larger over the years until it was mythical in size, rolling over common sense, including his own? Were Lincoln's words and actions taken to justify the most inane thinking? Didn't the Vietnam war teach him anything? What a fool he had been, he thought, to swallow hook, line and sinker the notion of innocence and the grandeur of questionable actions. Maybe he didn't know Lincoln's words at all, hadn't figured them out yet. No, he thought, he had. He was just enraged that no one seemed to pay attention to Lincoln's words, words that should remind us all of the human costs of war. Tears again flowed for the price his son had paid.

Charles didn't like himself when he got cynical. It wasn't his nature. He had become skeptical of people and events. Darlene told him not to worry, that a healthy cynicism was not bad. That was a long time ago.

◆ ◆ ◆

The sun was winding down across the sky casting its orange glow across the Memorial as the day ran its course. Thousands of people were sitting on blankets and sections of chairs across the grass of the Mall. The dome of the Capitol Building was lit up —

red, white, and blue. It seemed the whole capital was adorned with the patriotic colors. Charles stood at the top of the stairs looking at the lights coming on across the Mall. He looked at his watch. It read 5:59 PM. The steps to the Memorial were already full of jubilant people waving their flags. Charles would close the Memorial just long enough to allow him time to mop the floor.

SIX

While cleaning the floor, Charles spoke again to Lincoln as he might have with an old friend. He stopped to wipe the sweat, again. His shirt was wet, stuck to his chest and back. He pulled it away from his body.

"Had a full house today. 'Bout as big as McClellan's body guard. All wanted to know what you're thinking."

"You making fun of my public opinion baths?"

Charles easily assumed Lincoln's tenor voice. "The people don't want much and don't get much and they must all take their turn just like at the barber shop."

"Well, Abe, people are a little more demanding now-a-days."

During his work Charles kept up a running dialogue with Lincoln. "In case you were wondering, I'm pretty darn miserable. My wife thinks my skull is made of the same stone as yours. When times try a man's soul, the man drives his woman crazy."

The sound of another low-flying helicopter caught him off

guard for a moment, and he looked out across the Mall watching the helicopter speed past.

"'Work, work, work.' Isn't that what you say? 'Keep movin', don't want old age catchin' me,'" Alice said, laughing as she came out into the Memorial. Perhaps Charles' willingness to talk earlier gave her an opening. "Don't you think it's time to quit? Henderson just called. He thinks there's a code red coming." There was no response from Charles. "Take in a movie?"

"Seen 'em all," Charles said without stopping.

"I know how hard this day is for you."

"Go watch the fireworks," said Charles, continuing to sweep.

"Code red's fireworks enough for me. I'm going home," Alice said, but she didn't move.

"So go . . . or find a broom and make yourself useful."

Alice retreated back to the shop. A moment later the noose landed at Charles' feet. She gave a curt smile, retreating once again. Charles tried to ignore the noose. He pushed it aside with his broom. On the next pass, he picked up the noose, started to dump it in the trash, reconsidered, and jammed it in his back pocket.

Alice returned with a broom, joining Charles in sweeping up. There was silence, except for the general tremor of the mass of people lining the Memorial steps. A loud firecracker jolted both of them.

"Tell me that's just some fool getting an early start," said Alice.

Charles didn't answer, his eyes on the broom ahead of his quickening pace.

"You're the kind of man Lincoln liked," Alice continued, "not just because you clean the bird doo and the dirt behind his ears. You're a good man, Charles. Your wife's a lucky woman. I've known you a long time. I've seen you get well from a bad war, get stronger, smarter, be a good provider for your family, but working

48

double shift's not going to cure your loneliness, not going to bring your boy back. You're walkin' around with a hole in your heart. Time ain't goin' to heal it. This ain't no bad dream you're gonna wake up from. I know you don't want to hear this, you don't want company but you told me to get a broom. Just pretend I'm sending you an e-mail. You don't have to answer. I don't like to read 'em anyway. That's why I use e-mail so I don't have to listen to no reply. Guess that's why you talk so much to the man here in the high chair."

Charles' head moved ever so slightly but enough for her to know he was listening.

"Oh yeah, I hear ya. I like the way you do his voice. You should've been an actor. It's good 'cause he don't answer unless you do it for him. That's the kind of man I like. I know you been hurting. I lost my nephew over there. Wish I could tell you why your son had to die or what he had to die for. People so sure they're right, there's no more room. So talkin' stops and war happens. So what else is new. Poor souls like your boy get caught up in all that righteousness."

Charles slowed the tempo of his sweeping. Without looking up, he said softly, "Go home. Go."

Alice looked at him for a moment, concerned for her friend, and then turned and left just as another loud firecracker split the silence.

Charles finished sweeping and gave the floor a damp mopping. He spoke to Lincoln as he picked up a piece of paper from the floor. "People don't know how to pick up after themselves. 'Case you're wondering, there'll be no parties, no celebration, no back-yard barbecue, no birthday cake with sparklers. My boy's dead for no good reason, and we still got idiots walking around with nooses on their ties."

He pulled the rope noose from his pocket and looked at it. It was well made. Somebody took some time to do this, he thought.

Charles descended the people-infested stairs of the refreshed and clean Memorial. At the base, the Musician was back playing a harmonica this time. He smiled at Charles, who noticed a sign tied to the Musician's cart. It was printed in multicolored crayon: "Keep to the rhythm, and you won't get weary. Keep to the rhythm, and you won't get lost."

Charles knew that was what his mother had taught him, but he couldn't process it, couldn't find any rhythm, had lost all desire to go on. He loved his boy so much, had invested so much of himself in his boy. Richie had been a happy, loving child. Charles had pushed him to be all that he could be, to be the best he could be. Had he pushed too hard? Charles was unrelenting, but he had wanted his son to be prepared for what lay in store for him out in the world. Charles knew navigating the temptations of the street would not be easy for Richie. He just hadn't thought of him in a war zone. Charles missed his son deeply. He kept looking at the sign on the Musician's cart like a man trying to remember something.

◆　◆　◆

Richie had done most of the research for his American history class on school computers. Finally, Charles and his wife managed to buy him a computer of his own, and Richie had shown Charles how to use it. The boy wanted to work part-time to help pay for an internet hook-up, but Charles wouldn't have it. He didn't want his son having any excuse to be detracted from his school work.

Richie came out of his room like a bullet, carrying his laptop.

"Listen to this. Your great-great grandfather was a runaway

slave. He was recaptured or kidnapped and taken back to Georgia, but he escaped again, and that time he filed a lawsuit in Missouri to stay free. Yes!"

"A lawsuit? All right!"

Son and father had high-fived each other. Darlene had joined in the celebration.

"The original papers are on file in St. Louis, Dad. My teacher says they'll be on exhibited here at the history museum. We'll get to see them, plus the slave records, when they came over. Who owned them, all that stuff! Turns out we all descend from some tribe in North Africa somewhere. It's in our DNA, our genetic code. You're related to the president, Dad."

"We don't claim him as family," said Charles, wearing jeans and a Princeton University sweatshirt.

"No! The man. Your man. President Lincoln! Too bad he didn't know we're all related, huh."

"Hear this, Mom," said Richie reading from the internet. "Lincoln had a doctor named Samuel Howe look into the colonization of slaves to find some way to deal with all the freed slaves once Emancipation came to be."

Darlene smiled at her husband. They had both loved these moments with their son.

"I believe Dr. Howe was married to Julia Ward Howe. She wrote *The Battle Hymn of the Republic*," Darlene said. "She was also against the war."

"Anyway," Richie continued, "this Mr. Howe wrote to a man at Harvard asking his opinion about the freed slaves. Well, this Harvard guy said that interbreeding of whites and blacks would be a disaster. You hear that?"

His father nodded, smiling at Darlene as Richie again read from the internet. "The Harvard professor said the government should stop the mixing of races any way they could. He was really against intermarriage. This guy was at Harvard! You believe that?"

"Yeah," laughed Charles. "So what's new?"

Richie was rather dumbfounded by what he'd learned. He continued reading.

" 'They,' meaning us, 'are not capable of living on an equal basis with whites.' You're excepted, Mom."

Richie couldn't get over the fact that the man who said this went to Harvard. He was warming up to his ancestral research.

"So this Mr. Howe writes back and tells the Harvard guy that there are already more mulattoes in the country than there are just regular full-bloodied black folks. The Harvard guy didn't have an answer for that. He didn't want to do anything that would bring them, the whites, down to our level. Our teacher said Lincoln agreed with the Harvard man—that we were inferior. That's why he didn't free the slaves sooner. But if he'd known we were related . . ."

"You gotta cut Lincoln some slack," said Charles.

"Why?"

"Different times."

"No excuse."

"Besides," Charles said, "Lincoln was looking for answers, trying to keep this country together. He had a big problem on his hands, dealing with all those freed slaves, no jobs, no money, refugees."

"Listen to this." Richie scrolled down his computer screen stopping when he found what he was looking for. " 'I believe there is a physical difference between the white and black races which I believe will forever forbid the two races living together on terms of social and political equality.' This is Lincoln talking. 'And inasmuch as they cannot so live, while they do remain together there must be the position of superior and inferior, and I as much as any other man am in favor of having the superior position assigned to the white race.' "

"Lincoln was just trying to . . . he was catering to the white vote."

"Yes, he was," agreed Richie, "but he really felt that way."

"No, Lincoln did the best he could," said Charles after a long pause.

"He was a dictator, Dad. He could have woken up one morning and said, 'I think I'll free the slaves today.' "

"He did free the slaves. He was born dirt poor, no schooling, grew up to be president and freed the slaves."

"Lincoln was a segregationist. His picture doesn't belong on our wall with Reverend King."

"You don't know what you're talking about. King loved Lincoln. He spoke at Lincoln's Memorial. I was there."

"Just because Reverend King gave a speech there didn't make it a church."

"Some people think it is a church," replied Charles.

"Well, King would never have been here if it had been up to Lincoln because all of King's ancestors would have been in Liberia."

Charles could only shake his head and give a slightly exasperated look to his wife. Darlene had smiled. Richie asked his dad why Lincoln and others before him had not taken a stronger stance against slavery. Then he answered his own question. "Maybe they were all too comfortable because they benefitted from slave labor."

"Not Lincoln. And he wasn't a dictator." Charles adamantly defended Lincoln.

"He went to war without telling Congress," said Richie with the assurance of new knowledge."

"It was an emergency," said Charles defending Lincoln.

"He arrested people, held them without a trial. He blocked ports, took over railroads, confiscated firearms. Just try that today. They can't even get guns away from kids at school."

"Lincoln *freed* the slaves!"

"But he still wanted them out of the country."

Charles looked at his wife.

"I'm out of this," she laughed.

"Your husband's in trouble," Charles said.

"You got to find the good stuff, Dad, not the puff stuff. The good stuff's on the internet."

"Are you just going to stand there?" Charles asked Darlene, waving his white handkerchief. "Can't you see my S.O.S.?"

"Stop picking on your father," Darlene teased.

"I'm picking on Lincoln. He didn't go to college, right?"

Charles shook his head, "No, but he wasn't happy about it either."

Darlene looked hard at her son. "Like your father, Richie."

"Your mother's right."

"That Harvard guy just reaffirmed what Lincoln believed. Lincoln had a low opinion of my intellectual prowess."

"Give the man a break."

"Lincoln thought that only the very brightest of blacks could vote. How do you know who's bright? That's why they came up with literacy tests."

"So," Charles said, "You're saying that Lincoln would have been pleased that the next hundred years and counting would be segregated turmoil?"

"Right."

Charles turned toward Darlene. "Will you talk some sense into your son?"

"Maybe you should take a refresher course on Mr. Lincoln," said a smiling Darlene to her husband.

Charles started pacing the room. His son was making him uncomfortable. "From people like that Harvard idiot," said Charles, his arms in animation, "who claim to be educated came the fear of the one-drop notion. One drop of black blood in the river would pollute the whole river."

"The Harvard man said we all come from different species, but according to my science teacher, Charles Darwin said we all descended from the same source, a common ancestor. The guy from Harvard would not be convinced. A mulatto could be a professor just like him, but he would be treated the same as if he were hanging out down on the corner. Our teacher says it's the same today."

"Let me tell you something that not many people know, including you," said Charles. "Lincoln had a valet, a man by the name of Johnson. A mulatto. The point is, he was a free black from Springfield, Illinois, that Lincoln considered a friend and treated him like one."

"A well-treated slave is still a slave."

Charles slowly nodded his head, conceding that his son had a point, but continued, "Lincoln paid for the man's funeral. He's buried out here at Arlington National."

Richie could see that his father was upset by his comments about Lincoln.

"It's okay, Dad. Lincoln pretty much gave up the idea of sending us out of the country after he issued the Emancipation Proclamation. I doubt if he had changed his mind, but he realized it would be very difficult. I wonder if Lincoln read Darwin's *On the Origin of Species*? It was published in 1859. None of it matters. One day everyone's going to be mulatto. The Harvard dude was as closed to science as Darwin was open. Darwin was right. Evolution is a fact just like gravity. Maybe it scares people to admit that we are all related. Certainly scared the Harvard dude."

"No wonder Cornel West left Harvard and went to Princeton," mused Charles as though a light flicked on. The Huggins family had followed the West story and his disaffection with Harvard closely because Darlene and Charles had read his books and those of West's colleague, Skip Gates. The men were considered two of the more prominent African-American scholars. Charles and Darlene had wanted Richie to be exposed to them.

"You can take West's class at Princeton," said Charles.

Princeton was a subject Charles would not let go. Richie had been an early admission to Princeton but for his own reasons refused to commit. He was on the "wait list" of several other top schools. Charles was convinced Princeton was the place for his son. He had gone so far as to filling out the application himself, but was stymied at the essay requirement.

Whenever he brought Princeton into their conversation, Richie clammed up and changed the subject or left the room. This day was different. Richie looked at his mother, then took a deep breath. "I'm not going to Princeton."

You could have knocked Charles over with a feather. For a moment, he couldn't speak. Richie knew how much this had meant to his father, and he hated himself for hurting him; but it was his choice, and he was going to make it.

"You . . . ah . . . I'm gonna have a heart attack. Princeton's begging for you. You're a rare man, son."

"What your father means, Sugar, is that you're male and more than qualified."

"And I'm black."

"That's right. Princeton needs you."

"Yeah," said Richie, lowering his head.

"Don't give me no 'yeah,' " Charles protested. He turned again to Darlene. "Tell your son he can't turn Princeton down. White southern boys used to take their slaves with them to Princeton."

"Stop nagging. He will do what he wants." Darlene laid her hand on her husband's arm, but Charles would not be deterred.

"He will do what he has to do — go to Princeton," declared Charles. "Anyone else in your class have a chance to go to Princeton? No. Not a prayer. Not half of them are going to graduate. And you know why? It's got nothing to do with IQ'S. It's because they think they might be accused of acting like 'whitey.' "

"Yes dear," Darlene said putting her arm around her son. "Oh, Charles," she laughed, "you sound like Bill Cosby."

"Dad, a lot of kids want to make good grades."

"Yeah, the ones without the three "R's" — Remington, revolver and reloading."

"Dad, listening to you talk about when you were young, I don't think the kids are much different. They still don't trust the police, they think whites got better schools, they don't like abortion, but they don't like making it illegal either."

Darlene looked up. "Thank you, son." She met her husband's eyes. "And Charles, I think most of Richie's classmates, despite how they feel about certain things, are pretty upbeat and most of them graduate," added Darlene.

"I know when I'm outnumbered. All I know is, you better get educated if you want a bank account — or a car. Don't follow the crowd. People believe what they want to believe. You do your thing. Knowledge is freedom. An engineer equals a bigger paycheck and more respect."

"There are no black engineers," said Richie matter-of-factly. Charles couldn't believe his ears. He was speechless.

"Who told you that?" This came out of Charles like a popped cork.

"My college counselor," muttered Richie.

"What does he know? That's stupid. He's stupid." Charles was pacing around the room waving his arms. "World's full of black engineers. Don't follow the knuckleheads. You do your thing." Charles was beside himself.

Darlene put her hands up for Charles to stop. Richie started to leave the room. Charles blocked his path.

"Let's settle this right now."

"Charles."

"Can you give me one good reason why you don't want to go to Princeton?"

"This conversation," Richie said. "Dad, there's no way I'm going to feel comfortable at Princeton. Everybody will be looking at me thinking they know why I got in. I don't want to be on display, some ivy league . . . ornament."

"What are you talkin' about — ivy league ornament? I'm not asking you to be Princeton's house nigger."

The "n" word made Darlene see red. "That word will not be uttered in this house, not by anyone, including you!"

"It's just a word, Mom," said Richie.

"It's a disgusting word."

"Kids use it at school all the time. It's *how* you say it."

"I don't care how you say it, it's wrong," countered Darlene.

Richie, mildly reprimanded, returned to his room.

"What kind of counselor tells a kid that?!" Charles was quiet for a moment. "He's got a chance to go to Princeton."

"It's not so easy for him. Someone called him 'token boy' at school," said Darlene.

". . . What does that mean?"

"They think he got in because . . ."

"He's black," Charles said.

"Pardon me?"

"Privilege is now on my side."

"It certainly took long enough," said Darlene, hugging her husband. "Privilege didn't make it safer or easier for Richie at school."

"So, what if he did get in because — which he didn't. I don't understand."

"They call him 'schoolboy.' "

"I don't care what somebody calls him. They're idiots. He's got the grades. Who cares what they think? I'm just asking him to take advantage, that's all."

"He says Princeton will still be there."

"After what?"

"After he gets out of the Marines . . . please. Richie wants to enlist in the Marines." She knew how Charles would react to this news. "He didn't want to tell you. He thought it would be better if I broke the news."

"Well, he's not falling for that 'few, the proud and mighty' crap. He wants to throw his life away? Not in that cess pool we got no business being in. He's done everything right. He's on the way, Darlene! Marines? Over my dead body!"

Charles shut the door behind him.

SEVEN

Charles pulled out a one-dollar bill from his wallet and dropped it into the Musician's hat. The Musician bowed, and his twinkling eyes followed Charles walking away down a pathway.

Charles walked along the reflecting pool trying to avoid the crowd, which was practically impossible. Concessionaires were selling ice cream and sodas — anything cold on a hot humid evening. Vendors were hawking flags, patriotic knickknacks of all shapes and sizes. Charles never ceased to be befuddled by the seemingly endless boisterous commercial aspect of this thing called freedom. Extricating himself from the perplexing web, he let the mass of people rush by to find a place to watch the fireworks while another helicopter passed low overhead. Looking for terrorists, Charles thought. Looking for a needle in the haystack.

At that instant several firecrackers went off behind him giving him a jolt. A tropical jungle with soldiers patrolling flashed in his mind with the loud drone of the chopper's blades.

60

A soldier pokes the body of an enemy with his bayonet. Satisfied the enemy is dead, the Viet Cong soldier walks away. Slowly the body moves, the eyes open. It's Charles as a young soldier, but the young soldier's image quickly changes to that of his son, Richie.

Charles continued walking through the Mall and the multitude of July Fourth revelers celebrating America's birthday. It didn't jibe. How, he thought, could these people be so jubilant?

"They had free elections all over Iraq," argued a passing young man to his companion.

"Yeah," said Charles without looking back, "they had free elections in Vietnam, too."

◆　◆　◆

When his son announced his intention to enlist, Charles had no clue about Muslims. Where was Iraq? All he knew was all his mother had known when he told her he was going to Vietnam — that it was on the other side of the world.

The Vietnam War was all still so close, yet illusive, nothing Charles could put his arms around, like dissipated Fourth of July fireworks. The nights that he awoke screaming were long gone, but the nightmare was still there, still very real.

Charles had been in Vietnam in 1967. He had some faint recollection of hearing something about elections, but he was too busy trying to stay alive. Since Vietnam, Charles had learned of necessity to be more improvisational about life, to adapt, to court skepticism, if he was going to be able to cope with a future. He didn't want his experience to happen to his son.

His son's enlisting in the Marines and being sent to Iraq was

Charles' own story all over again, opening up old wounds, wounds he had suppressed for a long time, had paid a dear price for. Vietnam had put wounds in his body and a hole in his heart. When his son was set on becoming a Marine, there was no choice. Charles would have to deal.

In a last desperate attempt to dissuade Richie from enlisting, Charles decided that he would try to explain to his son about Vietnam, about a war nobody liked but where everybody thought they were right. Some people were so convinced, there was no room for those who thought differently. The inevitable result was a war where conversation had stopped, where the ones killed or displaced were usually the ones caught in the web of others' righteousness. They were almost always heart-breakingly young soldiers — like Richie.

Charles had never wanted to reveal his war experiences. He had never told Darlene or Richie what he'd gone through. He couldn't bring himself to read any of the countless books written about his war. He never joined any of the veteran groups. Yet the Vietnam War that he hated had defined the rest of his life, even more than being black had.

"We've done our duty," he told Richie.

It was hard for Charles to acknowledge that he never knew what his war had been about. It was harder trying to explain his feelings about it to Richie.

"I have no idea why all those soldiers died. For what, I don't know. I know I just can't forget. I came to terms with it. Time helps do that. I had really looked forward to serving in Vietnam. Government said you had to be there. Guess I was a patriot. College wasn't a choice for me. That didn't matter 'cause what I wanted was to be a hero, a warrior, an all-American boy, the cavalry to the rescue. Had no idea where Vietnam was or why a war was being fought. Never gave a thought. I had no idea what lay in wait. All that jungle training went out the window that very hot and sticky first day in 'Nam.' "

It didn't take long, Charles told Richie, to realize the jungle of Vietnam was a place he was going to hate, a place no one would tell him anything about. "I was as ignorant as a pile of dirt, as ignorant about the jungle war as the freed slave was about freedom. The jungle training we received didn't prepare us for the realities of jungle warfare. I had no idea what was going on. Never asked. Just tried to survive."

"You did," said Richie.

"I was lucky. I felt alone over there, such an awful lonely feeling, let down. It was a mess. My being there was all for naught. I was fighting the wrong war. How could I continue? I lost my beliefs. A man without beliefs is a lost man, a devastated man, a man who can't act, can hardly move. I did my job as best I could, as did fellow soldiers. You killed or were killed. That was our world."

Charles' disillusionment with Vietnam, he confessed to his son, began to wear him down until he discovered that to not care why he was there, to have no cause, was actually, ironically, making him a better soldier. He was braver, more alert. He decided feeling too strongly about something led to carelessness when emotion would overcome instincts and common sense. He cautioned his son about emotions.

"I know, Dad, I know." Richie laughed. "I know I'm young, but I know."

Charles wondered about his son's state of emotions right before he was killed. Had they betrayed him?

In Vietnam, Charles quickly assumed the mad-dog role. How fast the veil of innocence lifts when one sees the brutality of man. Darkness was abundant.

"God was nowhere in sight. I volunteered to be the point man for my company, the one in front who hopefully keeps his troops out of trouble. It was stupid 'cause you would likely die. But at least I could trust myself not to fall asleep."

It had been a cover for fear, but soon Charles' fear was replaced with a cold, hard, scary calm. A strange peace. Thereafter he was never again afraid but always on edge.

"I was a killer. I had learned my job well. I had paid attention in training camp because you would be in trouble if you didn't."

This was about death and destruction. This was all out bloody war. But what the hell, this was better than home. Willie from Philly reminded him, "You could just as well be shot in the street. Besides there's no jobs and no future there. So how bad can this shit be?"

"Was it really that bad at home?" Richie asked.

"Willie said it was. Perhaps for him, it was. Home was so far away. Yeah maybe some folks were afraid to leave their houses for fear of being shot."

He couldn't remember now. Vietnam had not been a place for reflection, but Willie had, he remembered, gotten him to thinking about the dangers back home.

"I remember hearing gunshots late at night when I was a young boy. One time when I left for school, I walked past a dead body. He had been a neighbor. The hall of the apartment building was full of blood.

"You still don't like me walking to school," said Richie.

"Yeah. My mother told me once not to play with my squirt gun in the street 'cause in our neighborhood someone might think it was a real gun."

Charles gave a little laugh. As a child this was hard for Charles to understand. Not so for Richie. There had not been many occasions where young Charles had been aware of danger, but Richie knew how dangerous the streets of D.C. could be. He knew that in his school anything that looked like a gun meant suspension.

Richie was a captive audience, glad his father was opening up to him. He prodded his father for more.

"What about your war buddy, Willie from Philly?"

"Willie was a little older and more battle-seasoned. 'We're just slave masters,' he'd say, 'trying to oppress the people. What's the difference between us and the crackers back home?' "

"There is evil, Dad. That is what must be oppressed."

Charles had no answer. In Vietnam there had been no welcoming crowds, no greetings with thankful arms. It was somewhere in the Vietnam jungle that Charles lost respect for life. It was all a horrible murderous waste, killing people because they didn't wish to live the way you wanted them to. Where is the high ground in that, he finally wondered?

Still, although Private Huggins had lost faith in what he was fighting for, he had compassion and respect for his fellow soldiers. That his enthusiasm had slowly faded for any "cause," Willie told him, was good because his early enthusiasm would probably have gotten them killed.

The rule was not to leave your foxhole unless ordered.

"Stay planted. Stay alert," Charles told Richie. "If you were black, Vietnam was a good spot to release all the rage that you were carrying. The problem was I wasn't carrying any rage. Like I said, I just wanted to be a hero, serve my country. I thought it would be as good a job training as any. 'At least you'll know how to kill,' Willie joked without so much as a smile. I couldn't read a map when I got to Vietnam." He lowered his head saying, "And I didn't have anything personal against the Vietcong."

"When I came home from Vietnam, the world seemed different. Washington, D.C., was different. The country was different. I was different. The war had put a big hole in my life. My beliefs and ideas were tattered. I'd believed in what I was sent there to do, but the country wasn't backing me up — little did I know. Got squeamish, second doubts. You want to be a world power, then shut up and do it. The war destroyed a lot of things. A young man's self-viewed idealistic way of life was simply gone. I forgot what life had been like. You, son, brought that lost youth back to me." Charles put his hand on top of his son's hand.

"War takes your innocence. When I was a senior in high school I brushed up against a hard reality. When segregation ended, I found myself at a predominately white high school. I lettered in four sports at that recently integrated school. Made All-State in all four, but there were no scholarships, aside from all black schools. But I was welcomed with open arms into the marines, so that was where I went with all my fire and ideals. Guess what I'm trying to say is that you have a choice, son."

"All-State, huh? How come you never told me?"

"I don't know. When I went back to visit the school twenty-five years later, the high school's sport trophy case was full of trophies that I was largely responsible for. But there was no picture of me to be found. No name either."

Charles was still for a moment.

"What happened to me, I don't want it happening to you. My life had suddenly . . ." He looked away toward the window groping for words that would never begin to express what he had faced as a young marine. "My life was changed . . . horridly changed, and I was no better for it. Vietnam was not the road to a better place." He looked back at his son. "Is Iraq the road to a better place?"

"Don't worry about me."

"That's what dads do. What else?"

By then Charles was almost pleading with Richie to reconsider his decision. A thunderstorm had come up during their talk. The clap of thunder distracted Richie from his father's impassioned words. Charles felt the thunder as explosions all around him. He was exhausted, but he was determined for his son to hear all. It was a confession of sorts.

It was more than Richie wanted to hear, but he listened as his father tried to trace a world that had become closed after World War II. A world that had become less tolerant in its desire for more discipline and less naivete.

"Didn't want another Pearl Harbor. Tolerance and freedom were said to be respected during this time. But tolerance was only skin deep and was easily shed for true feelings that vibrated just beneath the surface. Your grandfather found the door of tolerance closed tight."

Charles had no wish to follow the path of his daddy with no bank account, no car, no insurance, no teeth, no identity, no self-respect, no nothing. His daddy never figured out how to be black and American at the same time, but he had a lot of pride.

"He couldn't read, but you couldn't tell. He hid it."

His daddy would only laugh when he heard his little boy talk about what he had learned in school about Abraham Lincoln.

"Daddy laughed hard and long so that he wouldn't cry when listening to Leadbelly's song about Lincoln rising from the dead and bringing justice to the Jim Crow south."

" 'You can't eat justice,' he'd say. Daddy never stopped moving long enough to settle and belong anywhere. He had never found anyone to lend a hand."

"When were men ever equal?" asked Richie. "What are kings and emperors and dictators and popes about? We all want equality, but nothing's perfect. Lincoln wasn't. I think his idea of government 'of the people, by the people, and for the people' is something for the world to go for, and when we achieve that then we will have the freedom that Lincoln wanted. It's time to punt. Sometimes, Dad, you have to go for it. Maybe Lincoln was a dreamer."

"I don't think so," said Charles.

"Guess I'm a dreamer. Maybe that's why I enlisted."

Charles shook his head. Richie had a maturity, a view about things unusual for his age, Charles would brag to Darlene. How can you know so much at age 19? You can't, Charles thought. You just can't.

◆　◆　◆

Many tears were shed the day Richie left for basic training. They were the remembered tears for what the Vietnam War had taken from Charles. And now another war had taken the greatest and most cherished thing he ever knew — his son. Neither time nor the opening of heaven itself could heal the wound of his son's death. He had heard all the slogans.

"Slavery's bad, freedom's good."

"Freedom and liberation."

"Union and the people."

"Honor and freedom."

Alice was right. No one had a clue. No one could tell Charles why his son had to die or what his son had to die for. Would that he could have taken his place.

His son had been equipped with the latest in weaponry. He wielded a brand new bayonet, sharper and stronger than older bayonets. It could double as a fighting knife. Its steel blade was eight inches long and almost an inch wide. The blade had a sharp point with serrations near the handle. There were no blister points on the handle. It was a lethal weapon that cost $36.35, and Richie told his father he knew how to slash an enemy diagonally from shoulder to hipbone. Abraham Lincoln, who was always seeking the latest in weaponry, would have wanted this bayonet for his soldiers. But this new lethal bayonet was no match for a land mine.

Charles wished he could bring himself to say his son's death had not been in vain.

EIGHT

Behind Charles was the innocent laughter and shouting of three boys running. The image of the noose flashed. Just then another helicopter circled low and loud overhead. He was reminded of an old Lincoln saying about a traveler in a stormy night. When thunder came crashing down, the traveler called out, "What we need around here is a little less noise and a little more light."

With all the candles on America's birthday cake, Charles thought there should be enough light for all to see.

A couple of homeless men were lounging on the grass. One of them had a milk carton on his head. For an instant, in the light fog that had settled, the milk carton looked like a stovepipe hat.

Looking back to the path, Charles saw a figure in the fog coming near him. He could make out that it was a gaunt man with a tall hat. Charles blinked his eyes. Five other men of various shapes and sizes in tall hats, wearing beards and black clothes, complete with bow ties, followed the first. The men were Lincoln impersonators.

A funny sight. The lead impersonator shouted back to the others, "Come on! We're late."

Charles could only shake his head. There must be some sort of Lincoln look-alike competition, he thought. The six men hurried on in their costumes. A straggler appeared out of the fog following the rest. It was the Musician dressed like the Lincoln impersonators with a fake Lincoln beard except his hat was the crazily colored Dr. Seuss hat he used to collect donations in. The Musician was whistling "Dixie" as he marched along after the other Lincoln impersonators, tipping his Dr. Seuss hat to Charles. Charles thought that if he never heard the song "Dixie" again, it would be too soon.

Backyard-variety fireworks went off in the distance. Charles walked around aimlessly for the next hour or so, not wanting to go home. He found a bench to sit on but soon grew restless, deciding he was better off walking.

Nearby was a newsstand he frequented. He browsed through the newspapers ignoring a headline, "Forty Killed In Baghdad Blast." A copy of the *Weekly World News* tabloid caught his eye with the headline: "ABRAHAM LINCOLN WAS A WOMAN." A picture of Lincoln in a wig and bonnet accompanied the article.

"Shocking pics found in White House basement."

"Who knew?" The vendor laughed.

"Who cares," replied Charles.

"Yeah. Everyone else has claimed Lincoln, why not the gays."

"Why not? It's a free world."

The vendor said he wasn't surprised that pictures had been found of Lincoln dressed as a woman. "You think it's true?"

Charles didn't answer, being amazed that people actually read those things and believed them.

"He was an ugly man," said the vendor, "but he was a better

lookin' woman than his wife. You ever see her? She took the cake for ugliness. You never see a picture of the two of them together — never. They had issues, those two."

Charles was aware that Lincoln had some marital problems, and he wondered if the problems might have resulted, in part, from the loss of two sons and the agony of the Civil War. The vendor took a closer look at the tabloid, nodding his head.

"Abe was a babe. It figures. He sat funny in those pictures — real feminine like, huh? And that beard looks fake."

Charles didn't respond. It was not a subject that interested him.

"Shocking," said the vendor.

Despite his disdain for the "rags," Charles plopped down fifty cents.

"You been working for a transvestite, Huggins. A presidential transvestite at that. Who knew Lincoln and J. Edgar Hoover had so much in common?"

Charles couldn't see the stairs of the Memorial now for the sea of people. None of them were concerned about terrorism. They figured that with Lincoln looking over them from his throne, nothing would happen. He glanced up at the Lincoln Memorial and then at the tabloid picture again of Lincoln dressed as a woman.

"This is what you get. This is what it comes down to."

He finally found an unoccupied bench and sat himself down. The night air had not made a dent in the temperature or humidity. He was feeling a bit woozy, so he stretched out across the bench with the tabloid across his chest.

The Musician wheeled his grocery cart down the path coming to a stop in front of the reclining Charles and glanced back toward Pennsylvania Avenue. The soft clip clop of horses hooves could be heard echoing down the path. The Musician started off with his cart, softly whistling "Hail To The Chief" as he went.

The road running along beside the Mall was full of cars heading to their sundry destinations. A horse-drawn carriage, shrouded in fog, pulled up to the edge of the sidewalk. A lone, tall, thin, bearded man climbed out of the carriage waving the driver off. The fog seemed to have thickened a bit more, the air heavier.

A moment later, the black-coated man ambled slowly and laboriously on long legs as though making his way to a funeral he was not anxious to attend. He made his way out of the foggy murk toward the reclined Charles.

Because of his height and manner of dress, the tall, gaunt man, his hands folded behind his back, was imposing as he stopped a few steps away from Charles. He glanced around as though looking for a place to rest his bones. Seeing no other seat, he removed his shawl and stove-pipe hat and awkwardly squeezed between Charles' feet and the end of the bench.

The tall man pulled out a handkerchief and wiped the sweat from his forehead. He then quietly took off his boots and rubbed his feet. The unintentional jostling woke Charles.

"I'm sorry. I didn't mean to disturb you. Needed to take a load off these bones," he said, continuing to rub his feet."

Charles sat straight up not sure whether he was awake or dreaming. Giving the man the once over, Charles thought he looked very much like Lincoln. Another impersonator playing the part to a tee. This man definitely looked like a winner. But his demeanor was in sharp contrast to the other Lincoln impersonators Charles had seen earlier in the evening.

Upon closer observation, there seemed to be nothing Charles would call joyful in this man. He was polite, but seemingly lost in his thoughts. Charles had seen many photos of Lincoln. All were stoic, but he knew photos from that era had dictated a rigid demeanor.

The tall man sat very still and quiet for a long time. Finally Charles tried to strike up a conversation.

"Hot, isn't it?" There was no response.

"You in the show?" Still no response. After several minutes it was evident that the man was not going to volunteer any information. Maybe he was not in the mood for idle conversation.

Charles was intrigued. He couldn't help noticing the man's face contorting into a deeply lined expression of grief as though in the midst of some terrible pain, some unspeakable burden, some awful decision to which there was no relief. Charles was not put off by the man's demeanor. He understood the dark side all too well, the loneliness of it, the neediness of it. He found it refreshing that there was no polite phoniness to this tall replica of Lincoln. This man was the picture of gloom itself. He must be a good actor, Charles thought. Must be getting paid for his representation, probably by the Park Service to entertain the tourists.

This man might be going overboard, though, Charles thought, in his portrayal of Lincoln. He had read about actors becoming so absorbed in their roles that they had a hard time shedding them.

The man rubbed his feet again, and his mood seemed to lighten. The morose demeanor had disappeared. The dark cloud had passed, and he finally spoke, "It's always hot this time of year in Washington," said the man wiping his neck with a handkerchief. "Downright miserable. I don't like it. We try to get out to the Soldiers' Home as much as possible to get away from the heat and the hustle and bustle of the office. My wife's out there now. I come in every day."

Charles could only nod his head, thinking that this fellow was too much. He was really in the role. Charles looked at the tabloid and chuckled. The man looked at Charles' face for the first time.

"Laughter's such an elixir isn't it, no matter how modest. I mean it's a matter of survival. Laughter, that is."

Charles nodded again, not quite knowing how to respond.

"I suppose," Charles mumbled. He couldn't remember, though, the last time he had really laughed out loud.

The tall man's curiosity got the best of him.

"If you don't mind my asking, just what is it that's tickling your funny bone?"

"I do mind," Charles said, not meaning to be so abrupt.

"Oh, well, as the lawyer said, 'I have no business here, but I have none anywhere else.' It would be interesting to know exactly what I have done to cause you to laugh in my presence. I realize my appearance can be off-putting, but usually people refrain from laughing out loud."

Charles reconsidered. He felt bad. The man was probably just trying to earn a few dollars imitating Lincoln. The man's eyes were kind. His face was deeply lined, as if he'd aged beyond his years though his hair was coal black.

"Since you asked — because of a picture of you."

The tall man seemed taken back by Charles' remark. "Oh, and which picture would that be?"

Feeling a bit uncomfortable, Charles started to get up though his eyes strayed back to the tabloid showing Lincoln posed as a woman. Again he chuckled — at the absurdity of it all.

"I suppose you've seen this," he said, holdling up the paper.

The man shook his head.

Charles felt a little foolish, going along with the man's charade, but this "Lincoln" was so committed to his adopted persona that Charles found it was diverting his attention from his own despondency.

The tall man let his long legs stretch out full before him, tucked his handkerchief into his pocket, and pulled a paper and pencil from his hat. The man tapped the pencil to a blank page, appearing to think to himself.

"Writing is good therapy, and it often saves me from myself. I find it good to write something and leave it — not send it at all."

There had been times when Charles had certainly wished he'd not *said* certain things, but that was water over the dam.

Charles noticed the man's unusually long arms. He looked at the picture in the tabloid again, comparing the picture to the man's face sitting beside him. The man's hair, when he had removed his hat, was wild looking, as Lincoln's appeared in some photos. Charles thought the man could use a little grease and a stocking cap he'd seen his father wear a few times. Even the famous mole on Lincoln's face was in the right spot on the man's face, and Charles couldn't help noticing the man's rather high-pitched, reedy voice with more than a bit of a drawl to it.

There was another long silence and just as Charles turned to leave, the man said, "Well, though I don't know about a photograph of me that might bring you to laughter, I'm sure there are many, and I'm glad to have enhanced the humor of this July Fourth night air."

Charles looked again at the tabloid and handed the paper to him.

The man was having trouble comprehending what he was looking at. He stared at the photo, gradually realizing, with some astonishment, what confronted him.

"Oh, it's me," he said, then commenced laughing so hard his whole body seemed to shake, a volcanic spewing of laughter. Charles was astounded at its ferocity.

"This is a definite," his laughter interrupted him, "improvement. My wife will be impressed. Ah, I am especially fond of the bonnet."

With that he erupted again in laughter, his knees rising to his chest. Charles had always tried to get beyond Lincoln the myth to the real man, but he wasn't prepared for this . . . this raucous laughter. He mused that Lincoln as a woman was as close as some would ever get to the real man.

This Lincoln was now delighted. His load seemed lighter, if temporarily so.

"Laughter is the better medicine. This . . . this object . . . is just the ticket. I needed a good chuckle," he said, handing the tabloid back to Charles. " 'Course if I was a woman, the Maker may have made me just as ugly so I would have no reason to be tempted," and he burst out laughing again.

Charles wondered about a man who would laugh so hard. As suddenly as this Lincoln erupted into laughter, he quieted into somber again, as if in some deep gloom. He bowed his head as though in prayer, his elbows resting on his knees, his hands cupping his face. Charles thought he heard the man say he was not well. He couldn't be sure. He didn't look well. Charles decided he would take a chance and try to lighten the mood.

"This 'rag' said people mistook you for a man because you had so much facial hair." Charles leaned into the man asking, "Is that a real beard?"

The man was surprised at such a question but quickly recovered, taking no offense at Charles' question.

"It was, last time I checked." He then gave a pull on his whiskers. "Truth was, I had at first questioned whether people would think a beard was silly. But after growing it, I happened to like the beard. It gave me a little needed dignity. What do you think?"

"It fits you."

"I'd always been clean-shaven 'til I ran for president."

"Anything for a vote," Charles said going along for the ride.

"The taste was in my mouth a little."

"Certainly," replied Charles with a touch of sarcasm.

"I'll have you know that a little girl told me she thought I would look better with a beard. Her name was Grace Bedell. I have her letter right here."

Charles had been familiar with this bit of Lincoln history so he was curious as to what the man would say. He was astounded when the man pulled a rather fragile looking letter out of his stove pipe hat, opening it up quite carefully. It was apparent to Charles that the man had chosen this prop with the greatest care. The letter looked so authentic he must have spent much time in choosing just the right letter, much like Lincoln, he thought, had done in looking for the right word — not just any word — but the right word. Charles thought of the care Darlene used to take in choosing a hat. "Not just any hat," she would tell him when he questioned why the process was taking so long, "but the right hat." Anyone, Charles decided, who had gone to this amount of time and care in creating something was not to be dismissed.

The man was obviously pleased with the letter and commenced to read from it: "You would look a great deal better for your face is so thin," he read to Charles.

"She was right, best political advice I ever got. The Republicans liked the beard and it was hard for them to agree on anything . . . like putting a couple of lawyers in a room together, there's sure to be an argument. Anyway, little Miss Bedell said all the ladies liked whiskers, and they'd tease their husbands to vote for me. So I grew a beard. My face is a little gaunt. Some New York Republicans said that whiskers would help my look."

Charles was now convinced this fellow was a heck of an actor. On closer observation, he noticed the man's high forehead — he was a dead ringer for Lincoln.

"Maybe *you* should grow a beard," the man said to Charles. "Your face is a little thin."

Charles did not acknowledge this with anything more than a shrug. He was not comfortable with the conversations being turned toward him, but he was becoming intrigued with the man's manner.

"You wore a disguise when you came to Washington for your inauguration. You dressed up as a woman."

For a moment, Charles thought he saw a false note in the man's impersonation. He became somewhat agitated, then quickly recovered. This man knew his part remarkably well. Hardly missing a beat, he impatiently explained he had worn a hat and cape on arriving in the Capital. "The State Department tried to tell me what to wear. I wasn't about to be blackmailed by the secessionists nor was I going to be intimidated by any threats on my life. I'd sooner been hung on the steps of the Capitol than to give in to any threats of disruption to the inauguration."

Just then two well-dressed, very exotic young women, one of whom was black, passed in front of the man and Charles. As the ladies walked by, the man's face lit up. He stood up a little awkwardly, straightened his coat and adjusted his tie, then realized he had forgotten to put his boots back on. Charles noticed the man's eyes following the women as they walked away.

"My wife doesn't tolerate other women very well," he said, sitting once more. "Although I received an interesting letter the other day from an anonymous source asserting my wife was very friendly with a certain young fellow who has been helping her decorate the White House. I laughed, but come to think of it, she has made a few trips up to New York — spending too much money and maybe not all of it on furniture." He seemed to take delight in the thought. He told Charles a story about a woman who came upon him on one of his walks. " 'You are the ugliest man I have ever seen.' I told her that I couldn't help it. 'Well,' she said, 'Maybe you can't help it but at least you could stay home.' "

Charles noted he began laughing before he got to the punch line. He stopped laughing when he realized that Charles wasn't. He explained it was a joke of sorts. He then quoted a stanza from a short poem he said had been written and published in a newspaper in 1860.

> Any lie we'll swallow.
> In any kind of mixture.
> But don't we beg and pray,
> for God's sake show his picture.

"It was making fun of my ugliness."

"Ugly's good," Charles assured him. "You can't take a handsome president seriously. You don't trust him."

The man got a chuckle out of that. "By that reasoning, I must be the most trust-worthy man in town. I can sort of laugh now but I was very self conscious of my appearance as a young man."

"You look like the boss undertaker in your get-up."

They both chuckled.

NINE

After a bit "Lincoln" rose from the bench, and the two men walked in silence. They came upon the Lincoln impersonators on a make-shift stage. The Musician was there in his Lincoln "do." The audience was laughing at the various Lincolns. Charles noticed that the man beside him seemed dismayed.

"They say imitation is the sincerest form of flattery," said Charles.

"I'm not used to flattery so I reckon I should be grateful. I've endured a great deal of ridicule without much malice, and received a great deal of kindness, not quite free from ridicule."

"Welcome to the club, Mr. President."

"You don't have to call me Mr. President."

Charles was getting a bit tired of this charade. "Well, ugly or not, you're the President, and I can bend and bow with the best of them. Born to serve. Bless the Lord, jubilee, Father Abraham's come. Glory hallelujah." Charles found himself kneeling in front of the man.

"Don't . . . don't kneel to me," said the man uncomfortably, stepping back.

Charles got back to his feet, a little taken aback by his own behavior. It reminded him of Willie from Philly, his take-no-prisoner Vietnam buddy.

The man seemed unsure what to make of all this, but he couldn't help noticing a tinge of sarcasm coming his way. He let it slide as easily as his long legs kept pace with Charles.

Charles checked his emotions, reminding himself that this fellow was just an innocent actor doing his job.

"Just call me Lincoln," the tall man said.

"Sure, and you can call me General Grant," quipped Charles. Still, the man seemed so genuine . . . "Why should I call you Lincoln?"

"Because that's my name."

"All right, Lincoln it is." Charles gave a salute.

"No need to salute," said Lincoln.

"Yeah, enemy see me saluting you, they'll know who to set their sights on. Tall bird like you would be sniper bait."

Lincoln didn't comment.

They passed by the Vietnam Memorial Wall. After all the years, it still brought the war back into sharp focus for Charles. The names etched on its granite face were a powerful visual, and they drew him in emotionally. Despite the pain it brought back, the Wall had been a healing force for Charles. Though it didn't change his feeling that soldiers had died without reason, at least their names were recognition for paying the ultimate price.

"If crazy folks want to get at me, no vigilance can keep them from it. With Vice-President Hamlin being such an ardent anti-slavery man, he is an insurance on my life worth half the prairie land of

Illinois. I've never thought there was a man alive who would do me any harm."

"Death's the price you pay for underestimating the enemy," Charles said, continuing to walk. He noticed that Lincoln looked as tired as he looked sad. He decided it seemed right that Lincoln should choose to wear so much black. "We both seem to have that fault — melancholy. We're two sides of the same coin," said Charles.

"Melancholy," Lincoln explained, "is a misfortune, not a fault."

Charles contemplated Lincoln's remark as they walked. "Well, we must be two of the most unfortunate souls here tonight."

Lincoln looked into the distance. "There is more of discomfort than real happiness in existing anyway, even under the most favorable circumstances."

"So what's your advice?" Charles asked.

Lincoln considered the question for a moment before answering.

"It's what I told a little girl who asked me to sign her book,

> You are young, and I am older;
> You are hopeful, I am not.
> Enjoy life, ere it grows colder.
> Pluck the roses ere they rot.

Charles didn't say that his son never got the chance to grow older. He also gave up the idea of trying to out-pace Lincoln, and he was in no shape for a run.

"How long are those legs?" Charles asked.

Lincoln looked down and then without a hint of a smile said, "Long enough to reach the ground." Then he laughed.

"I'm not used to seeing high brass in the field," Charles said, recalling those who stayed in Vietnam just long enough to get their ribbons and then were on the first plane out of there.

They were now nearing Pennsylvania Avenue. The fog was lifting. Lincoln looked up at the street sign. "The other day a boy threw a stone at a dog on Pennsylvania Avenue and hit three brigadier generals." Again Lincoln commenced to laughing, enjoying his own humor. Charles looked blankly at him.

"I would die if I did not have my jokes," Lincoln said almost apologetically. He looked up through the trees to the emerging full moon which lit up the White House in the foreground.

The shadows through the trees took Charles back to his night patrols as lead soldier in Vietnam. The shadows played tricks. The enemy was out there; he just couldn't see them. The V.C. would be hacking in on the radio frequency telling them to go home. The V.C. always knew where they were. He thought of what he had told Richie, "The enemy you can't see is the most dangerous. Soldier needs a target he can hit."

"A soldier needs a cause," said Lincoln.

Charles was weary of the word, having lost his son for a "cause."

"This can be a dangerous place," Charles said to Lincoln. "You don't walk here at night, even with a full moon."

Lincoln motioned toward the White House, "I think it may be more dangerous over there."

"You may be right," agreed Charles. "They just don't realize how dangerous they are. They say you're sitting over there with them, walking the halls, whispering in their ears. So I guess there's no need to worry. Your ghost, you know, haunts the place."

That brought a laugh from Lincoln. "I feel like a prisoner over there," Lincoln said, motioning again toward the White House. "One end's full of lodgers, the other end's on fire."

Abruptly Lincoln changed the subject. "This was cattle grazing land."

"This mall was a forest. Slaves cut all the trees," said Charles, pointedly.

"Yes they did."

If Charles expected more, he was disappointed.

"Have you seen a stray goat out this way?"

Pointing to the Capitol, Charles told him, "No, but I've seen a few old goats up there on the Hill."

Lincoln stopped and laughed. "Tad's goat is gone. He's upset as he loves that goat."

"Is that the reason you're out here? Looking for goats?"

"No," Lincoln said. "No, just trying to figure out what to do."

"About the goat?"

"About everything. I do some of my better thinking at night, especially when I'm walking. It's quieter to have the noise of the day set aside. And when I have work to finish, I cannot sleep."

"I haven't been sleeping so well myself," Charles allowed.

"It's just a great relief sometimes to get away. I hate staying in the old room by myself. Nothing but business, which is tasteless to me. I need company. I dropped by Secretary Seward's, which is just around the corner, but he wasn't in. Don't know where he went. Maybe the theater. He's always going, doing something. I need some company."

"Not mine you don't," Charles mumbled.

TEN

Charles was understandably feeling hungry, since he had not eaten all day. Truth was he hadn't eaten a good meal in months. He found himself and Lincoln sitting at the counter of a small snack shop known to the locals for good food and generous proportions served up by the owner-cook, a fellow Vietnam vet. It was a place much like the barbershop Charles frequented, a sort of "soapbox" where people used to not being heard, feeling unappreciated by the greater public, could vent. Nothing much ever got settled, but people felt better if they were able to get certain "gripes" off their chests.

There was a banner hung on the wall behind the counter that read HAPPY BIRTHDAY USA. There were some framed caricatures of past presidents including Washington, Jefferson, and Lincoln. Lincoln liked being paired with Washington and Jefferson. He told Charles that one of the first books he read was about Washington — "an inspiration he was, partly."

"Which part? The aristocratic part or the sense of entitlement part?"

Lincoln said, "The brilliant part, the part that served his country like no other. He was pretty near perfect."

Charles didn't respond further to Lincoln's remark about Washington, being ambiguous about his feeling for the first president. He stared blankly as he took a sip from his cup of coffee. The cook was a big man with a messy apron and a chef's hat. He was sweating profusely while talking to a customer.

"It was a Katrina cleansin,' that's what it was." Ain't been so many blacks on the move since Lincoln freed the slaves."

Then he turned and saw Charles. "Look what the cat drug in."

The cook turned back to the patron. "Lincoln knew. He took it to 'em. Full court press."

"Wife and I saw Lincoln in that . . . amusement park?"

"Disneyland."

"That's it. Deep voice, real manly, like some movie actor."

Lincoln leaned in closer to Charles "Amusement park?"

The patron said he'd heard they tried to replace Lincoln with Kermit the Frog.

"Nah," said another patron, "Kermit's just a frog. Lincoln was the president."

"Maybe Kermit oughta run for president."

"He did," responded the cook.

A good time was being had.

The cook bent over the stove. "Goin' to be a My Lai night. Heat's killin' me. Ain't doin' you no good either," he said to Charles. "You look like death warmed over and your friend needs some meat on those bones. I warned you. White folks can't cook. It's a sad reality. Everybody knows that." There was laughter as another helicopter zipped loudly overhead. The cook looked up. "That whup, whup, whup gets you every time. They can't train the ears." He kept up a running monologue while working the stove. "Findin' a terrorist out there tonight's like lookin' for a virgin in a brothel. Look at you, you're wastin' away. Good food takes the proper ingredients. Not that fat free stuff. It's like honest-free conversation. You get my drift? No taste, might as well be chewing rubber. Look at these fixin's."

The cook spooned up sausage, biscuits and gravy, grits and greens surrounded with baked corn, a piece of fried chicken with mashed potatoes and gravy. He piled Charles' plate with enough food for a week. Lincoln asked Charles if this might be his last meal. Charles didn't answer but just looked straight ahead. Finally he said, "This is like the meal my mother fixed the night before I left for boot camp. Then I was too excited to eat. Tonight . . ." He couldn't finish whatever it was he might have said.

"This is heart attack on a plate," said the cook as he slid the plate in front of Charles, who laid a couple of five dollar bills on the counter.

"Put your money in your pocket. Been taken care of over there. The cook nodded to a man seated at a table. It was the Musician, who acknowledged Charles, who nodded in return. "He escaped the great New Orleans flood with the clothes on his back and his horn," said the cook, as if in confidence. "Horn's all you need if you're any good. So it'd be impolite to not eat up, not to mention an insult to the cook."

Charles was used to seeing and hearing the Musician every day for months. He had simply appeared one morning. The Musician never talked about the flood or anything else, not a word — at least to Charles. He let his saxophone do the talking for him. The devastation of New Orleans had hit the vulnerable Charles hard. Darlene had surprised him a few years back with a trip to the New Orleans Jazz Fest to celebrate his 50th birthday.

As he had watched thousands of black victims of Hurricane Katrina despairing on his television, Charles had wondered how far we'd really come from slavery. This country, he concluded from television and newspaper accounts, could sink from the weight of injustice and inhumanity. Lincoln, thought Charles, had known the danger to this country lay in those who were out of sight, thus out of mind. Charles never bought into the rumor circulating in his neighborhood, that the levees had been blown up by a bunch of skin-head racists. They were overlooking the power of natural events.

He took some solace in the amount of money donated—his own donation included. Danger lurked deep for the people living in the lowland of New Orleans. These people had suffered a grievous wrong. "How can anyone deny what's in front of their eyes," he had vented to Darlene. "These are hungry, desperate, angry, grieving black people. They look like the mass of freed slaves must have looked — going out of the dark into light — hopeless and abandoned. They got no notion, no means, no idea what to do." Charles had delivered this monologue to Darlene over breakfast one morning. " 'Course if you watched television, you'd think only black people suffered and died. There's a lot of rampant white guilt to take advantage of."

Charles noticed that Lincoln was only drinking a glass of water. He asked, "What do you feel like eating?"

"That's what I'm trying to figure out."

"How in the world do you ever make up your mind about what is the right thing to do, or say?"

Lincoln, looking slightly comical on the stool with his knees pressed against the base and his gangly arms stretched across the top of the counter. "Those kinds of decisions are no easier or harder than deciding what to eat. Besides, I find it hard to take my vittles regular. Not much of an eater. Kind of just graze around."

Charles recalled his son's letters saying how much he missed his mother's cooking.

"Once in the ranks, a soldier is rarely well fed," said Lincoln.

The cook wiped his hands on his apron and took a gulp of water. "Glad you're here, Charles. Look around. You got a lot of friends. You can't blame yourself, can't feel guilty about what happened to your boy. You can, but it ain't going to do you no good. Lot of blame to go 'round. Slave traders, slave masters, they go back 500 years. I was just readin' it. The worst are the ones who promise and don't deliver. There's a whole list: educators, political leaders, the president, me, you — we're all in the guilt game."

Charles frowned. Even before he lost his son, he wasn't into "blame" sessions where the plight of black people was endlessly tossed back and forth, looking for reasons why things were the way they were.

"And the racists," the cook laughed. "You gotta love 'em. Findin' a good racist with deep pockets is like hittin' the lottery. I been waitin' for a good racist to sit down here for twenty years. Can't blame yourself . . . . You never were much of a talker."

"Good conversation's not easy."

"Neither's good food. Now, eat up."

Lincoln asked Charles, "Did you enlist?"

Charles gave him an incredulous look.

"Drafted?"

"You mean chased?" asked Charles.

It had seemed to Charles that every friend he had in high school had been "chased." Many of them had been sent to Vietnam.

"The enemy drives every able-bodied man they could reach into the ranks, very much as a butcher drives bullocks into a slaughter pen," said Lincoln.

"Except the wealthy ones who wiggled and bought their way out. I don't believe your son was drafted was he?"

"No, his mother couldn't . . . he went to Harvard. Then he served with Grant."

"Behind the lines."

"Yes."

Charles didn't press the issue further.

"Nobody had to chase me anywhere," lamented Charles. "I enlisted. I wanted to go — fool that I was." Richie's face flashed again before his eyes.

"You in the field?" asked Lincoln.

"Yeah," came the soft answer, then the question, "You?"

Lincoln nodded. "Captain of the Illinois Volunteers."

"Was that like the Salvation Army?"

"Blackhawk War," Lincoln answered.

"How long you in for?"

"Fifty-one days," Lincoln shrugged. "You?"

"One year, two months, four days and three hours."

"That enjoyable was it?"

"Yeah."

Charles asked Lincoln if he had seen any action.

"Made a few charges upon some wild onions. Had a good many struggles with the mosquitoes."

Charles appreciated the self-depreciating remarks. He told Lincoln the toughest fight of his first night in the field was against the mosquitoes — "darn little creeping, crawling, buzzing, screeching dive-bombers."

Lincoln smiled and said that after he was mustered out, "my horse ran away and I had to walk home."

Charles took another sip of his coffee. "I would've walked home if I could've."

"A deserter? Well I guess if God gives a man a cowardly pair of legs, how can he help their running away with him?"

The humor of the line escaped Charles. He asked Lincoln why he had pardoned so many deserters.

"Just trying to get out of the butchering business."

"Didn't bother General Grant," Charles mused.

"My wife would certainly agree with that assessment," said Lincoln, "though I believe it was an undeserved assessment."

"Deserters or generals, we're all niggers in the field."

Charles got the intended reaction as Lincoln's brow furrowed. "I suppose that's one way of looking at it."

"There is no other way. Same mud, same blood, same can of beans. We're all alike, right? Equal, right?" Charles let that set a moment. "I mean . . . dead all look alike, no matter what color. Smell alike too, friend and foe, smell of death's the same. We're all brothers in war, Mr. President. It's peacetime we got trouble, just can't leave well enough alone."

"So much destruction . . . . misery," Lincoln said.

"Killing must not be too bad, there's so much of it," Charles responded.

The conversation wasn't easy, and it was blessedly over. Both men had lost their appetite. Charles looked around and saw that the Musician was gone.

A loud burst of fireworks broke the stillness.

"Those fireworks can put tears in my eyes," said the cook. "Fourth of Julys can be hazardous for us old vets."

ELEVEN

The streets were calm as most people had gotten to their destinations. A few stores were still open. The federal buildings were all closed, the workers having the day off at their homes in the suburbs. All the restaurants seemed full, mostly of Washington insiders wheeling and dealing. It was the tourists who celebrated July 4th. Charles was aware of Lincoln beside him.

"You're going to miss your parade. I don't need company."

"You left your change on the counter," said Lincoln waving the two fives.

"Honest Abe."

"I try to do right by people."

Charles looked at him. "Thank you." Charles pointed at Lincoln's image on the five-dollar bill. "You see that fellow there?" Lincoln peered down at it for a moment, then he smiled.

"Yep, that's you," said Charles.

"Well, I'll be," Lincoln replied, rather pleased. He studied the picture. "It's a likeness different than most."

"Bad hair day."

"Every day," smiled Lincoln.

"You got a good grade of hair. Little axle grease, stocking cap, you'd be clean as a whistle."

Lincoln held the five-dollar bill at each end, holding it taut to get a better look. He nodded appreciatively.

"You like that, huh? Guess who's on the ten."

"Who?" asked Lincoln.

"How should I know," said Charles "I'm lucky to have a five! Don't bc greedy. You're lucky. Washington's on the one-dollar bill."

"Where's Jefferson?"

"In bed with his slave."

Lincoln let Charles' comment slide still looking at the five-dollar bill. "I wanted from the earliest times to accomplish something, to link my name with something that would be of interest to my fellow men. That was what I desired to live for. I guess a five-dollar bill is of sufficient interest. What's your desire?"

"I have none."

Lincoln considered Charles' answer for a moment and then asked a rhetorical question, "Who would put this poor, lean, lank face on anything?"

"You don't know the half of it. You're an industry."

"Why?"

"Why do you think?"

"Money."

"Bingo."

"Money's the rub."

"That's what happens when you become a legend. Country was up for grabs, you were fighting for union and liberty, and then there was that untimely event on Good Friday. Now your face is all over the place, carved in a mountain."

Lincoln seemed perplexed. "I'm not used to flattery so it comes all the sweeter, I think. A mountain?"

"Yep," Charles went on. "Your name's all over this country — cities, towns, cars. You're big box office, a log-cabin industry."

Charles stopped at a phone booth and flipped through pages of the phone book. "Lincoln Bar and Grill, Lincoln Bus Lines, Lincoln Savings and Loans, Lincoln Elementary School, Lincoln Plumbing and Home Repair, Lincoln Pest Control."

The last one amused Lincoln. "I need that one."

"Lincoln this, Lincoln that, Lincoln ad nauseam," said Charles.

"Too many pigs for the tits," said Lincoln.

They walked down a street lined with several businesses. Charles was explaining the theory behind using a name you can trust as they passed a Lincoln Savings and Loan Company. "Yeah, they put your name and face on a sign, add one of your homespun quotes . . ."

"Homespun quotes?" Lincoln was not happy.

"Yeah, like Betty Crocker, Peter Pan, you know."

"No I don't," Lincoln said curtly.

"They think it's a slam dunk. They sell illusions, illusions of equality, honesty. You know about that, don't you? People buy something for the way it sounds, you know, the short annals of the poor kind of thing, the rail splitter image. People don't hear what it actually says. You see, Lincoln, it's all in the packaging. It's everything."

"The more modest the gift, the more grand the wrapping," concluded Lincoln.

Just then an older, well dressed African-American couple

walked by lost in their own conversation.

"I freed the slaves in the capital," said Lincoln, as he curiously watched the couple as they strolled down the street.

"All the slaveholders in D.C. got $300 for each slave."

"A good investment it seems," cautiously observed Lincoln nodding after the couple.

Charles noticed a group of young African-American boys emerge from a record store with Snoop Dogg and Kanye West posters plastered on the window beside one of the Rolling Stones. A sign in the window read "Gangsta Rap." The young boys were all dressed in the familiar uniform of the day: baggy pants, slogan emblazened t-shirts, and assorted ball caps. "They got fancy shoes but they're going to have a tough time pulling themselves up by their shoelaces with no education and no daddy. Some things don't trickle down. Some people don't reach down."

Lincoln nodded as he watched the boys, remembering his own haphazard manner of dress with ill-fitting clothes when he was young. "When you don't have money, you have to use your freedom of imagination. You told me I looked like the undertaker. Being tall, I was always concerned about my appearance. Those boys look pretty good to me. They got a hop in their walk." Lincoln's attention was riveted on the young men.

"Yeah, now it may be that some would laugh at your get-up, but the shoes and hats those boys are wearing may get them robbed or killed. Kids today have to pay attention to what they wear. If you're a black kid, you've got to be careful about the color you wear. That's no joke. My boy couldn't wear certain colors. I wouldn't let him."

Lincoln didn't know what to make of Charles' comments. They continued down the street past the record store, stopping in front of a Nike store where posters of Michael Jordan, the basketball player, and Tiger Woods, the golfer, and various other sporting stars, most of whom were black, lined the windows. Lincoln was fascinated with their pictures. There was a Oakland Raiders' football jersey in the window. Charles recalled reading a story about a gang that had adopted the Oakland Raider jersey because of the Raiders' "outlaw" reputation. That jersey had been off limits to Richie.

"They're smiling," Lincoln said.

"You would be too if you had their money," Charles remarked matter-of-factly. "They're even bigger industries than you. If there's a million dollar bill, one of their faces is probably on it. But of course you wanted their ancestors in another country."

"I thought they would be happier."

"I'd say they have several million reasons to be happy," laughed Charles. "Don't get the idea that just because Tiger and Jordan are doing just fine that the picture is all rosy. Far from it."

That the picture was not all rosy did not surprise Lincoln. "They, Jordan and Tiger, are examples of progress, of the possibilities that can be, and their contributions add, I'm sure, to the nation's strength."

Lincoln was fascinated by a pair of Air Jordan athletic shoes in the store window. One of the shoes was sliced in half so that you could see the inner construction. Pointing to Jordan's poster, Charles told Lincoln, "I read somewhere that you were noted for your jumping ability as a young man, but this man could fly." Lincoln wasn't sure what to make of this, but he was impressed. "And Tiger," said Charles pointing to the poster, "he's a golfer. He marches through Augusta like Sherman through Atlanta, burning up the course, taking no prisoners. Takes his game right to them, shows them the blood and guts of a sand wedge. Death is mercy."

Lincoln was still concentrating on the shoes.

"I'll wager that those shoes could help a man's attitude. I'd like to try a pair of those."

A short time later Charles and Lincoln walked out of the Nike store with Lincoln sporting a new pair of Air Jordans. He had his old boots under his arm. He was definitely feeling lighter on his feet. There was a bounce in his step. He liked the shoes. He did a couple of hops to test them out. "These shoes make a man want to dance."

"You know if you had had your way those shoes might never have been. My son said you were no Reverend King because his ancestors would have been scattered to the winds or at least to Liberia if your idea of colonization had taken effect. There might have been no Michael Jordan because you wanted to ship his ancestors hither and yon."

"I truly thought it would be better for both races to separate," said Lincoln while lingering outside the store window, again studying the posters of Jordan and Woods. He could not get over how spirited the athletes looked.

"They're Gods—like you, Lincoln."

"Me?"

Charles took out the five-dollar bill, "See where it says 'In Abe We Trust?'" Lincoln squinted his eyes. "Right there," said Charles placing his finger on the bill where he wanted Lincoln to look.

"It does not say that. It says 'In God we trust.' "

"Same difference," laughed Charles, walking on.

"My director of the United States Mint put 'In God We Trust' on there. I let it be."

"You believe in God?" asked Charles as Lincoln strolled along.

Lincoln didn't answer. Finally, he said he reckoned God had

99

some design in mind for events. "It's up to us to carry out that design. I am intrigued by this biological evolution." It was evident Lincoln was not going to say anything more. He was not used to talking about such matters, didn't care to.

"Well, in this country, we make our gods. It helps convince ourselves how great we are. Last, best hope and all. Your war is won; your truth goes marching on. 'Course we're always surprised when you disappoint us. We put you up there in the high chair of greatness away from the maze of the common man. The kind of man people profess you to be, a man of deep feelings, religious feelings."

As Lincoln and Charles made their way down the street, Charles showed Lincoln the five-dollar bill again. "You see that real small print?" Lincoln had to put on his glasses. Still he was having trouble seeing whatever it was Charles wanted him to notice. He walked over to a lamp post and took a closer look.

"Reading is a very tedious business, particularly for an old man with spectacles, and the more so if the man be so tall he has to bend over to the light." At last Lincoln could make out the tiny letters on the five-dollar bill "Lincoln Memorial." Lincoln was somewhat confused. "A temple?"

"Yeah, you see that person sitting there in the middle of the columns?"

Lincoln squinted as he looked up.

"That's you."

TWELVE

Lincoln was truly confused and stunned at what he was seeing. They were standing in front of the Lincoln Memorial. There were still a lot of tourists milling about in the afterglow of the day's festivities. Standing at the edge of the reflecting pool Lincoln whispered, "It's a little grand for a country boy, This temple is a long way from my home at 8th and Jackson in Springfield, Illinois. How could I possibly live up to this?"

Charles knew Lincoln had struggled his whole life to live up to an ideal. An ideal that Charles' son had said Lincoln did not attain.

"This is impossible to measure up to," said Lincoln looking around at the massive structure. "I desperately wanted to be remembered, but this is far more than I could ever have hoped for, more than I could possibly have imagined." Motioning to the mingling tourists, Lincoln, his head bowed, said, "Don't they know I lost more than I won?"

"They don't care. A few believe they're 'born again' when they leave here. They love you, so lighten up."

Looking around him, concerned. "This was the Potomac flats, swamp land. That . . . ." He couldn't find a description apt enough for the Memorial to him. "It could sink." His concern was real.

"It has 36 columns, one for each state when you were President."

"But the swamp. They could snap like toothpicks."

"The foundations go deep — down to reach bedrock. There's a 45-foot-high subterranean chamber supporting this Memorial. A Congressman pushed for years to put a museum down there to house all your words."

Lincoln shook his head. "Least it smells better than it did. The smell from the sewage was like a thousand rotten eggs."

"Come on, Lincoln, let's get through all your adoring fans."

Some people were exuberant in the presence of the Memorial. Others were quietly prayerful. Charles and Lincoln made their way through the crowd, heading up the stairs.

"Your statue's made from the finest blocks of Georgia marble."

"Jefferson Davis would not be pleased," Lincoln said, grinning.

"I've gotten a chuckle over that myself," replied Charles. "Tennessee provided marble for the floor, Alabama's marble is on the ceiling, and Colorado's covers the exterior."

Lincoln could only stare up at himself.

"This statue would astonish and amuse a good many, especially my cousin Charles Hanks who felt my only accomplishments were jumping and wrestling." Lincoln walked around the base looking up at his sculpted likeness. "It's often said I'm tall, but I'm not quite that tall."

"That's what happens to legends," said Charles.

"Actually I used to be taller . . . but that was before the war."

102

The enormity of it all seemed too much for Lincoln, and tears rolled down his cheeks. Charles thought that perhaps Lincoln, like himself, had been afflicted with the notion that he may not have achieved what he wished to accomplish.

"Maybe this Memorial," mused Charles, "is vindication for all the criticism you have endured, a kind of reward for enduring the tortured self."

He watched Lincoln gather his emotions and continue his walk around the statue. A park ranger was talking to some tourists about the Gettysburg Address, what it was like the day of November 19, 1863. Lincoln commented that he didn't think many heard his speech that day, a speech he had been anxious to deliver. He had said to his friend Lamon, "I don't think this speech will scour." He said he couldn't recall much of Edward Everett's speech except that it was well received, though he thought it a little long-winded.

"Everett," he told Charles, "wrote me a note telling me he liked my speech." Lincoln looked at the south wall where his Gettysburg Address was carved into the marble.

"Promises, promises," said Charles.

"The promises are a devotion to freedom," said Lincoln. "Democratic government was at stake. If the rebellion is successful, then others will question whether our form of government is practical." Lincoln recalled, when asked to deliver a few remarks at the dedication of the grounds at Gettysburg that critics thought he was unequal to the task. "Said I was too clownish." He was used to such criticism. "At times it gets pretty ugly. My way is considered foolish and risky. My views are not very popular in some circles. I was and am an 'Ugly and ferocious old monkey from the wilds of Illinois who would bring in brutality, moral filth, and arbitrary power.' "

Charles laughed and then quoted from the speech, " 'The world will little note, nor long remember what we say here. . . .' Wrong! People have been quoting your words right along, especially politicians. Most folks know about your Gettysburg speech. I don't know that they give it much thought one way or the other, but you haven't disappeared like some. Maybe they think you're a little dangerous."

"Dangerous?"

"Yeah, some may be afraid the promises you've made will come true, will be redeemed."

"They should be. The promises are no more than a devotion to freedom, a new birth of freedom."

"You said that."

"If I said it ten times would they believe the eleventh?" Lincoln ambled across the Memorial and saw his second inaugural speech carved on another wall. He spent few words describing his feeling, "Looking around here, I almost forget where I come from."

He was, indeed, a long way from New Salem village in central Illinois, a stone's throw from the town of Petersburg where he had surveyed as a young man and a few miles from the capital of Springfield. "I'm afraid this is beyond me. I don't feel the least deserving." The Musician was playing *Barbara Allen*. "That's one of my favorites," said Lincoln. The ballad seemed to perk him up. The Musician then played a few bars of *Battle Cry of Freedom*. Lincoln gave a big smile. "I've become rather passionate about music."

"You're that well-meaning white man everyone wants a piece of," Charles told Lincoln. He asked Lincoln if he really split rails, knowing Lincoln was famous for his rail-splitting image. Lincoln said he wasn't overly fond of the image or of splitting rails. "Couldn't stand it to tell the truth. I split a few when I had to. When my father made me."

"A few?" Charles laughed. "Rails all over God's creation are worshiped as Lincoln artifacts. People have made a lot of money out of your rail-making." Charles continued laughing and recited, from memory, the poem that had made fun of Lincoln.

> Tell us of his fight with Douglas
> How his spirit never quails,
> Tell us of his manly bearing.
> Of his skill in splitting rails.

"The rail-splitting image helped you get elected. You didn't mind it then."

"No, 'spose not," answered Lincoln.

Lincoln strolled around the Memorial looking into every nook and cranny. "You know, I was born in a log cabin."

"Yeah, I know you were," said Charles. "One of the first things I bought for my son was a set of Lincoln Logs. They still sell them, making money off you left and right. Everybody knows Abe Lincoln was from the lower walks of life, an humble lad born in a log cabin and hopelessly poor. You were an oddball who read books by candlelight, raised yourself up in the world by your own bootstraps, debated Douglas, became president, freed the slaves, and saved the union. I was born in a log cabin, too. We're in the same boat. Yeah, this day laborer could be sitting up there," Charles said, pointing up at the statue.

"Oh?" said Lincoln.

"Should be sitting up there," Charles said.

Lincoln nodded saying, "Maybe you should." He then quoted Shakespeare:

I have no spur
To prick the sides of my intent, but only
Vaulting ambition . . . .

"*Macbeth*," replied Charles.

Lincoln looked at Charles in surprise.

"I know Shakespeare as well as you, Lincoln."

Lincoln nodded his head as if he was considering a challenge.

"Go on, try me," challenged Charles.

Suddenly Lincoln became distant, very somber. There was a long silence between them.

Charles knew Lincoln had loved Shakespeare and was always quoting *Hamlet*, or *King Lear*, or *Macbeth* — maybe his favorite. Lincoln was also fond of *Richard III*, but loved *Richard II*.

"I figure I've read as much Shakespeare as any man, but that's not all I read," said Lincoln, but sensed he may have met his match in Charles. "You probably do know Shakespeare better. I am defective in education. My father grew up without any, and there was nothing to excite the ambition for learning. All my schooling didn't amount to a year. I still don't know much. What I do know, I taught myself." He looked up at his statue. "Books. They nourished me. Once I began to read there was no turning back. I had to leave. I wanted to leave." Lincoln turned away, his thoughts to himself.

"This country doesn't value education anymore," said Charles. "Oh, the Asians do . . . and some others." His voice trailed off as he thought of how his son had loved learning.

"A nation's education in peril is a nation at risk," said a concerned Lincoln. "Whatever price you pay for education is worthwhile, for the price you will pay for not doing it will be much greater."

Charles had not heard Lincoln say anything more heartfelt. He thought back to his mother. It was she who was always telling him how smart he was. That had given him a certain confidence that had since been misplaced.

"I guess if I had had a little more ambition," Charles said, "I wouldn't be leaning on a broom cleaning up after your visitors."

"May be that you are contented with your station in life?"

"The happy darky? No, that's a wealthy man's reasoning," replied Charles.

Lincoln asked, "Do you like being the President's keeper?"

"The hours are long and the pay's short."

"You're a good worker," Lincoln noted.

"A credit to my race," Charles said.

"I hold the value of life is to improve one's condition. Whatever is calculated to advance the condition of the honest, struggling laboring man, so far as my judgement will enable me to judge of a correct thing, I am for that thing."

"Well, hurray, because I want to be rich just like everybody else," laughed Charles.

"There are no laws to stop a man from getting rich. Ambition is a delicate balance," said Lincoln.

"Tell it to the corporations."

Lincoln recalled Brutus' reason for joining the conspiracy against Caesar — he thought Caesar had gotten too ambitious. "A dangerous thing. Ambition is all right if you keep a good rein on it and combine it with conviction. Then you have a pretty good soup."

"The soup's been watered down for most people. The concentration of wealth is numbing," said Charles, looking out across the Mall.

"We must all be free to run the same race."

"That's a nice sentiment. But we can't all be winners."

"That's so," replied Lincoln. "I'm not a sentimental man. The race of ambition was a failure for me, a flat failure."

Charles looked around him at the edifice that had been erected to Lincoln. "You'll pardon me if I don't feel too sorry for you."

"There was a time when I felt sorry for myself, but it didn't take me anywhere."

"No, I suppose not. Alibis are a man's bane."

"It's the hunger to better yourself that is the propeller."

"Lincoln, some felt you were a self-serving tyrant who was willing to destroy half the country for your own ambitions."

"You want to be free to make yourself what you will," said Lincoln with a bit of gravity.

"That's a nice thought, if you're male, white, and not a slave," replied Charles, thinking no matter how real racism had been for his father and somewhat for himself, a man had to rise above it or else. Charles' brother Terry had fought for change on the front line of the racial battle. Charles had wanted Richie to know about his uncle, about his commitment to racial equality, how his Uncle Terry paid with his life for that commitment.

"Here you go, rail-splitter." Charles tossed Lincoln the broom.

Lincoln toyed with the broom, looking a little awkward with it. He held it by the top end with his right hand and then lifted it parallel to the floor of the Memorial, holding this position for a few seconds. He then slowly lowered the broom and handed it back to Charles. There was a challenge in the air. Charles proceeded to lift the broom, but not without difficulty. His face strained red as he held it straight out from his body. Suddenly his arm fell limp, and the broom dropped like a rock.

Lincoln smiled. "I was raised to farm work, but I never cared much for physical labor."

"You're a politician all right." Charles groaned, massaging his arm.

"I left physical exertion as soon as I could. I had a lazy streak, liked to roughhouse occasionally, though."

"Workers should be able to rise to new horizons."

Lincoln gave a short laugh at having his own words thrown back at him.

Charles threw Lincoln the broom again. Lincoln caught it with his right hand. Charles then gripped the handle with his hand right above and resting on Lincoln's grip. Lincoln understood another challenge was in the offing. He then gripped the broom handle above Charles' hand. They continued this game quickly, exchanging grips up the handle until Charles' grip at the top of the broom handle left Lincoln with no room and nothing to grip but air. Charles presented Lincoln with the broom and cheerfully went off to get another while calling over his shoulder more of Lincoln's words, "All men are created equal."

The Musician, mingling among the tourists, was smiling. While Charles was retrieving another broom, Lincoln "hid" his behind his statue and sat down, leaning against one of the pillars with his knees pulled up. Charles returned to find Lincoln with a grin on his face and miming with his hands that he didn't know what had happened. He then laughed and got up, took off his coat and recovered his broom. Charles gave Lincoln a short primer on the proper "swing" of the arm to get some rhythm, "No, Lincoln. Swing your arm, forward, back. Use both arms! Push, pull, push, pull." Lincoln tried to do as he was told but wasn't very successful.

"You were right to spend your time with books. Your father was right. You never would have made a farmer or a worker. You were better off at political meetings."

"My cousin Charles would have heartily agreed with you. He was a Douglas man, short and cocky like Douglas — a couple of roosters. And like Douglas, he didn't see anything wrong with slavery spreading across the country like a plague. My cousin even wrote a letter expounding on his mortification of my laziness and how ashamed he was of me." Looking around at the Memorial, Lincoln said, "I wish he could see this place. I would pay top dollar to see his reaction. I wish my father could have seen this."

The Musician sat at the bottom of the steps. He smiled, watching Charles and Lincoln sweep, and accompanied their sweeping with the playing of his sax. Lincoln stopped to listen to the music. "I don't think I could make it through without music. Been moved to tears by it. I wonder if he plays the banjo? Suppose he knows *Jimmy Crack Corn?*"

Charles urged Lincoln to get back to work. Lincoln swung the broom while singing just a bit off key, "Jimmy crack corn and I don't care. Jimmy crack corn and I don't care. Jimmy crack corn and I don't care. The master's gone away."

Charles and the Musician glanced at each other and laughed.

THIRTEEN

Shortly after Charles returned from Vietnam, he and Darlene were married. Not long after the wedding, where his brother was best man, Terry was murdered. His body was fished out of a river in Alabama. Their mother bore her grief with dignity, but she found it difficult to find any peace at home. "A home without people," she said, "is not a home." She became a nomad like her husband, finding it hard to stay in one place for any length of time. Charles and Darlene tried to get her to stay with them, but she wouldn't. She would not impose.

Charles felt the unendurable loneliness his mother must have felt as he stretched out in his cushioned chair, still in his park uniform. The Glock sat on a table beside the chair. The television was on, and *CNN* was covering yet another suicide bombing in Baghdad. He rose from his chair, and sidestepping books that were strewn about the floor, he clicked off the television.

Lincoln was draped over a chair with his legs dangling over the side. He had removed his coat, making himself comfortable though he was not unaware of the gun. He shook his head as he read aloud from a book in Charles' Lincoln collection.

"Your reading aloud a little distracting."

"Helps me think."

"You like reading about yourself?"

"You collection is extensive," said Lincoln, not unpleased.

"A lot of ink's been spilled on you," said Charles, looking around at all the books about Lincoln he had collected. "There's a bookstore out in Chicago that's dedicated to you. That's all they sell, books on you."

"They must have family money," Lincoln joked dryly.

"Over 16,000 books been written about you. Some just rubbish."

Lincoln was not surprised. "I've spilled a lot of ink myself that some think is rubbish. I've tried to keep my speeches short. It wasn't easy. I think I've penned more words than Shakespeare."

"There's a truck-load of words written 'bout you, a lot of white-wash. To read most of them, you were the all American Boy Scout."

Lincoln's eyes shifted to the gun sitting on the table beside his hat. Lincoln, perhaps thinking to distract Charles from his thoughts commenced reading again. Suddenly he slammed the book down. "Dictator or king — rubbish!"

Recalling his son's words about Lincoln being a dictator, Charles said, "I was asked to fight a war because of you."

"Me?"

"Yeah. I ended up 10,000 miles away fighting somebody else's civil war, a white man's war, because of you."

"Me?" Lincoln seemed not to fathom what he was hearing.

"Yeah, you."

"What the devil were you doing fighting 10,000 miles away?"

"My president ordered me!"

"Suppose he ordered you to invade Canada to prevent the British from invading us?"

"You were the first president to call out the troops to fight an undeclared war, and everybody else has played follow-the-leader."

"They had taken seven states out of the Union, seized United States' forts, fired upon the United States flag, all before I took office."

"Yeah, yeah, yeah. 'If we don't stop the Reds in South Vietnam, tomorrow they will be in Hawaii, and next week they will be in San Francisco.' "

"That's hogwash," said Lincoln, with a dismissive wave of his hand.

"That was L.B.J."

"I don't know him, but that reasoning is as thin as homeopathic soup made by boiling the shadow of a pigeon that has starved to death! Like Polk and the Mexican War. Never heard so many words compressed into so small an idea."

"You haven't been around here lately."

"The outrage upon common right," Lincoln continued, "of seizing as our own what we have once sold, merely because it was ours before we sold it, is only equaled by the outrage on common sense of any attempt to justify it. Madness."

It was that same madness, Charles felt, that had cost his son's life.

"Reminds me of the farmer who said, 'I ain't greedy for land, all I want is what joins mine.' Polk's reasoning, like your L.B.J.'s, clearly proved to be false in fact, as you can prove that your house is not mine."

"You're getting off the subject," said Charles. "You were a dictator." Lincoln rose from his seat and started pacing the floor.

"You fired generals left and right," continued Charles.

"Those generals in the right have no cause to fear," said Lincoln adding rather scornfully, "and only those who gain successes can set up dictators."

"That's what Sherman did for you."

"General Sherman is good," said Lincoln, and then noted without rancor, "I don't let Sherman, or even Grant, make decisions about political matters, though both may think they are qualified. The President must keep negotiations in his own hands. A general's job is to give me a military success, and I will risk the dictatorship."

"You did. You suppressed publications you didn't agree with. You suspended habeas corpus."

"Only exercising emergency power — suppressing a revolutionary act, an insurrection against my authority."

"Yeah, what happened to Congress' authority?" Charles was shaking his head now. " 'Of the people, by the people,' I hear you. Didn't you close down newspapers, a whole bunch of them? Even Jefferson Davis stuck by freedom of the press. You arrested tons of people and held them without bail, you put thousands into the military, you paid others to recruit more soldiers, you spent the government's money, you blockaded the ports, took over the railroads, interfered with elections," and grabbing the gun, echoed his son, "and confiscated firearms! Just try that today." Charles could only think of Richie and wished he could have heard his dad take on Lincoln.

Lincoln, for his part, without the slightest change of expression, spoke in his calm, unimpassioned reasoned way. "It is my considered opinion that notions of my being a dictator are exaggerated. I have tried to be prudent and not be politically motivated. The nation's survival is at stake."

"Still," Charles wondered aloud, "what made you so certain that you were right in going to war?" Lincoln demurred for a second, "It was not me who was right. It was the Constitution. I took it at its word. The Union. It was older than any of the states. We the people of the United States are one, a nation. A man and woman can get divorced but not the country. We may live in different states, but we enacted a government for the whole nation. We needed to think calmly and well. We needed to take time to do this. Nothing could be lost by taking time. There didn't need to be bloodshed or violence."

This, Charles thought, was good advice that should have been heeded before his son went off to war. It seemed to Charles that this country was becoming just as divided as it was during both the Civil War and the Vietnam War. "But still, you were so sure of your belief that the union must be saved that in the end war was inevitable?"

"Unfortunately, yes," Lincoln acknowledged, "for where would we be? The question of union or secession could only be tried by war and decided by victory. There could be no compromise. Where would we be otherwise? A divided nation with the possibility of dividing into smaller factions with little or no power to serve the world. The Constitution, as Madison said, 'would be broken up and scattered to the winds.' That is what I wanted to avoid."

"You had to destroy the Constitution in order to save it," Charles mused. He had seen that happen in Vietnam and now in Iraq.

"The Constitution has not been abandoned during the war," Lincoln replied strongly. "Elections have been held even though it looked for sure as if I would lose."

"You had some hanky-panky going on . . ."

"Nothing serious enough to affect the election," maintained Lincoln. "You can never forego an election because the rebellion might claim to have already won. There was no overthrow of the government. The war has been fought to preserve our way of government, to prove that the founder's ideas of democracy could work. The Constitution does not allow secession."

"The only way to prove that was by killing each other?"

"Do you think the South would have given up slavery?"

"No, it didn't have to. You let Jeff Davis go. And you had no troops down there to make sure you got what you fought for."

Charles continued with another question, "Why didn't the founders do away with slavery when they had the chance?"

"A complex issue."

"Complex, my butt. They just didn't want to give up the life made possible by the slaves they owned. Did you believe slavery to be wrong?"

"Yes, a moral wrong."

"Then why didn't you give us privileges? Slaves could have made some folding money."

"I've always upheld your humanity and basic right to live your own life, the right of all innocent men to personal liberty."

"But you had no power over slavery in the South, and you had no intention of interfering with it."

Lincoln paused before answering, "I insisted the Union could not endure half slave and half free. It was my thinking — wishful thinking I admit — that slavery would just disappear or that it could be gotten rid of by legal and peaceful means. I was wrong. The North wouldn't have supported a war to free the slaves. I admit that southern resistance was deeper than I at first thought. If there was no union, slavery would have continued, and so what would have been the point? You, as an ancestor of slaves, know that an aversion to war could lead to an even crueler despotism."

"To win the war you threw the Constitution out the window when it was in your way. One of your generals arrested a man just for saying he wouldn't 'wipe his ass with the stars and stripes.' Another guy, drunk at the time, was arrested for saying he wanted to be 'the first man to hang you.' "

"Then he would have been the last man to hang me. There have been suggestions from everywhere you turn. To get away from it, I would have to take some rope and hang myself from a tree on the south lawn. Now that would make some folks very happy. My views are not very popular in some circles. Some of the Illinois infantry left. Some in the North felt a war would not be won. Some said it is unjust. Others said my friends would get rich because of the war. Others claimed I waged war against those who opposed my domestic and foreign policy. A few people felt slavery would eventually die out. To the supporters of slavery I was a fire-breathing radical, and to the abolitionists I was just an ineffectual hack, a Kentucky jackass."

Charles laughed and said Lincoln had nothing on him. "You're out of your league. Try 'coconut head.' " Another kind of challenge was on.

Lincoln gave Charles a bemused look and replied, "Illinois beast."

"Tap dancing fool," countered Charles. And so they went, rallying insults . . . .

"Butcher, animal, demon," boasted Lincoln.

"Loud, lazy, stupid."

"Pretzel, wet rag, coward."

"Savage, jiggaboo."

"Buffoon, gorilla."

"Coon, darky, nigger!" said Charles, emphasizing the final word.

Lincoln threw up his arms. "I don't like that word."

"Neither does my wife, but people don't hear that word; they think racism's gone away. You don't like the word "dictator" either, but you couldn't have gotten a sheet of paper of difference between you and a dictator."

"You have to consider the man behind the dictatorship."

"Guess this country's just lucky you were the president."

"You could've done worse."

"We have."

"It gets down to the question of must a government, of necessity, be too strong for the liberties of its own people, or too weak to maintain its own existence? I made the call. The people gave me their confidence, the power. I try not to abuse their trust."

"When is war ever over?"

"War ends when the defeated party says it's over."

"Suppose they refuse to admit defeat? The southern states ended up after you were finished with a way of life that was not too different from what they had before the war."

Lincoln was a little taken back by what Charles said about the South not changing its colors because if this were true, it meant the North had given back that which had been dearly paid for. It meant the North didn't have the will to see it through. Lincoln had been very aware that northern businessmen were more afraid of secession than they disliked slavery. He was quiet for a long time.

What Charles had learned from Terry was that so-called racial harmony had taken far too long. Terry's complaints would not wait for promises of solutions that his grandfather and father had waited patiently for. He wanted results now and was willing to become militant in his pursuit of results. Charles, a young soldier willingly in Vietnam, at least for the first months, found himself returning home to be on the outside of those young people like Terry who were against the Vietnam War and adamantly against politics as usual.

Ironically, Charles felt out of it in civilian life, too. He had to determine for himself where he stood on issues. When he first returned from Vietnam, he was a blank slate, but he knew his experience in Vietnam was not something he wanted to ever discuss. He knew little about politics; he was not anti-Semitic as some of his brother's associates were. Some of them were pro-Arab and against Israel in the Sixties. Interestingly, Charles' wife Darlene had told him that it was the Arabs who had killed vast numbers of blacks in Southern Sudan. "And no one lifted a finger," she'd said.

Charles thought the Jews and blacks should get along, having oppression and discrimination as common factors in their lives. This was something Charles remembered his father saying, "We can learn a few things from the Jews."

FOURTEEN

"This is where it all started," Lincoln said, pointing to a picture in the book he was holding. He closed the book and closed his eyes, reciting a poem from memory.

My childhood's home I see again,
And sadden with the view;
And still, as mem'ries crowd my brain,
There's pleasure in it too.

"You weren't raised in Georgia," said Charles. "Out the front door was town, what there was of it. Out the back door was nothing but Jim Crow and fields of cotton. My brother and I used to climb up in the rafters of this old barn and jump down into this big pile of cotton."

"And here you are." Lincoln grinned.

"Yeah, here I am." Charles looked toward his son's room. "God's will."

"There's a divinity that shapes our ends, rough-hew them how we will."

"*Hamlet*," said Charles, answering Lincoln's challenge. "Now what?"

"God helps those who help themselves," said Lincoln. Charles nodded.

"That why you wrote all those words, made all those speeches, fired all those generals."

"I suppose," replied Lincoln, his attention drawn to a photo of a woman with Charles. She was white, his arm was around her shoulders.

Charles looked at the photo of his wife. It reminded him of the day she left. It was raining. Charles had come home early from work. Darlene had written him a note and left it on the table. He'd picked it up and was standing by the window reading when he heard her enter the room. His hand fell to his side. Darlene was wearing a coat and carrying a suitcase.

"You know where I'll be."

"You fight for years," said Charles, thinking about his life, and trying to hold on to his emotions, "to get your act together . . . . Our son is dead! What for? A war nobody likes? Nobody cares about?" He looked out the window at some distant point. "The hardest thing was getting his things back . . . the Shakespeare book . . . in a box. What does anything mean. I can't believe it . . . ." He went quiet, finally without looking back to his wife, he said, "Go . . . just go."

As she started to leave, Charles said, "You don't understand, can't possibly . . . understand." As soon as those words were out of his mouth, he regretted them. If anyone understood him, it was his wife. His words had taken her by surprise. Never had she felt this had been an issue between them.

"Why? Because I'm white? That makes me incapable of possibly being able to understand?" She was tearing up, which was unlike her. "I think I deserve more credit than that. Our son would not have been pleased to hear you say that. I've loved you with patience and without judgment. I still love every bit of you. But my love's not enough." She turned to the door, but stopped, looking back. "Do you remember what I told Terry after he found out we were dating and was not happy about his little brother 'fawning over a hippy white chick who got her kicks hanging around black people?' I told him not all whites are slave traders. Besides John Wayne was not my hero, he was yours. I'm the one who introduced you to Miles Davis. I'm the one who gave birth to your child."

"That white woman is my wife. You have a problem with that?" Charles asked Lincoln. "You know, Frederick Douglass' second wife was white."

"Is that so?"

"Yep."

"Certain ideas lose their fashion," said Lincoln. "Such notions sort of run themselves into the ground."

"But you came out in some election and said you weren't in favor of black men inter-marrying with white women. Right? That's why you wanted us out of the country," pointing to the photo of his white wife.

Lincoln shuffled his feet.

"You think I was some black beast after your white woman? Were you protecting your manhood?"

"This is a game I don't care to play," said Lincoln.

"You were against a black man and white woman hooking-up."

"I was a politician trying to have it both ways. I lost that election you referred to. My opponent was insinuating that because I didn't want a black woman for a slave, that I must want her for a wife."

"And you didn't?"

"Not necessarily."

"Not necessarily? As a lawyer you must know that your answer is not beyond reasonable doubt," Charles said. "You remember those two women that passed by us earlier on the Mall?"

"Yes," replied Lincoln.

"Did you find them attractive?"

Lincoln thought for a moment.

"They were handsome."

"Men are handsome," replied Charles. "Those women were drop dead gorgeous, and one of them was black."

"She was?"

The two men looked at each other, and it was Lincoln who smiled first. "She was a whole lot of woman, that's all I know," Lincoln said, "and that is far beyond a reasonable doubt."

Lincoln picked up a photo of a group of soldiers. The soldiers in the photo were all black and all very young. It was disconcerting for Lincoln to see how young the soldiers were.

"We were young, full of fire, spit and vinegar, and innocence," said Charles.

Lincoln noticing a framed photo of a another young soldier. His uniform was different, but he looked a great deal like Charles. "Is this your son?" he asked.

Charles managed a slight nod. "He's dead."

"In battle?" Lincoln whispered.

Charles nodded again.

"He was everything in the world to me."

"I lost two of my sons. First, Eddie, then . . .Willie. We loved them so. They were such happy boys. Unrestrained by parental tyranny — in other words, they had the run of the house." Again he recited from memory.

> Oh why should the spirit of mortal be proud!
> Like a swift, fleeting meteor — a fast flying cloud
> A flash of the lightening — a break of the wave
> He passeth from life to rest in the grave.
>
> The leaves of the oak and the willow shall fade,
> Be scattered around, and together be laid;
> And the young and the old, and the low and the high
> Shall molder to dust and together shall lie.

Lincoln became too emotional to continue. "I'm afraid I'll have to save the rest till later."

Charles was glad, not because he didn't care for the poem, but it was too painful. He felt more like crying than talking.

"Is that one of yours?"

"I would have given all that I was worth, and gone into debt to be able to have written such a fine piece. It was penned by a Scotsman by the name of William Knox."

They sat for a few moments, each in his own thoughts.

"Looks like General Sherman went through this room," said Lincoln surveying the disarray. "Worse, looks like my office always did after my boys left." He picked up the scattered books putting them back on the bookshelf. "I'm not much of a homemaker," Lincoln said rolling up his sleeves preparing to wash some dishes. "This brings back my bachelor days."

"You ever pull all-nighters?"

"When I was on the circuit."

"Sleeping around with all those other bachelors were you?"

"My fellow lawyers."

"There's a rumor going around about you."

"That's not unusual," laughed Lincoln. "What's the latest?"

"That you're gay."

"That's nice because I've never considered myself to be a happy-go-lucky sort of man. But I enjoy a good laugh.

"That's not exactly what I mean." Charles thought Lincoln might be dodging the subject. "The talk is that you've been intimate with men."

"Yes, I suppose."

"Shared a bed or two?"

"We all did."

"You have known men."

"I certainly have."

"In the biblical sense."

Lincoln finally realized what Charles was referring to and commenced laughing.

"What if I was? After all, I am president of all the people."

"Just don't get any ideas, Lincoln."

"You know a man could get awful lonely in the wilds of Illinois." He gave Charles a sly look. Then Lincoln again started to convulse in laughter.

"My dear friend Speed would have had a good laugh. He and I shared a bed for three or four years. Close as we were, we never talked about such things." Lincoln noticed the Negro head salt and pepper shakers on the table.

"My wife collected some racial memorabilia. She wanted our son to know about past indignities. 'Course they're some who still don't give a damn how you feel," said Charles, now picking up a

125

towel to dry the dishes Lincoln was washing.

"How did you end up in Washington?" Lincoln asked as he handed Charles a glass to dry.

"That surprise you. That we ended up here?"

"Yes it does. I didn't think free blacks would move north."

"No, and that's because you thought we would all gladly pack up and ship out."

"The North would decide on its own to welcome you or not."

"What you're saying is that you opposed integration," said Charles.

"I am not one of those few who see a fully integrated society," admitted Lincoln.

"Well, they kept us down on the farm, so to speak, like you wanted. What kind of freedom was that? My grandaddy couldn't hardly go anywhere in the states but he was welcomed to leave the country. Daddy thought things'd be better up here, and if it wasn't — so be it."

"What will be, will be," said Lincoln.

"God helps those who help themselves," whispered Charles, repeating Lincoln's belief. "So we packed light — all we could carry — and here we came."

"Some northerners were afraid of that," lamented Lincoln. "Competition."

"Yeah, they're the ones who are offended by others' racism," said Charles. "There goes the neighborhood," he said as Lincoln handed him a plate to dry.

Charles recalled that his daddy's man was Roosevelt. "He was president a lot of years after you, a Democrat. 'Course after you, a Republican running for office in Georgia couldn't attract flies to manure. My mother could remember daddy singing, 'Mr. Roosevelt, you're my man. When the time come I ain't got a cent You buy my groceries and pay my rent. Mr. Roosevelt you're my man.'

"Daddy always felt there was something better just down the way. But no place wanted him. He hopped a lot of trains, uncomfortably crossed a lot of state lines, and walked down many roads, but they all dead-ended. Mama got tired of moving. Daddy survived as long as he could in the back alleys, and one day he gave up. He left and never came back. Got lost. They buried him back down in Georgia. He couldn't get away. I never thought he would set foot on red clay again. He hated Georgia — guess he figured he could hate it best if he was back down there. He must have enjoyed making them mad. But maybe all that time he was just trying to get back home. He was long in the ground before I knew he was dead."

"I didn't attend my father's funeral," Lincoln mused.

My father always said, "When you know something, really know, nobody can take it away from you. They can exclude you, put up roadblock after roadblock, call you nigger, and hang you, but they can't take away what you know. You carry it with you." Charles finished drying another dish. "I trust he did."

"What did you want to be when you grew up.

"A cheerleader."

"Well, I hold the value of life is to improve one's condition," Lincoln said.

"Jesus, I'm not serious. I wanted to be a cowboy."

"Why didn't you?"

"Because some fool told me all cowboys were white, and a bigger fool believed him."

Charles thought others had been fooled.

◆   ◆   ◆

127

He knew the years of slavery had branded a race of people. The Katrina tragedy had riled him. Darlene had listened. "If they're out of sight, they're out of mind. Now here they are for all to see. Someone will find a way to blame those poor souls for their misery. 'Get over it' will be the advice. If the Jews survived and flourished, then why can't the blacks? What good does that do except stir up trouble. The Jews did suffer, but they weren't held in slavery for hundreds of years, at least in America."

Charles knew all the statistics. He had rattled them off to Darlene and Richie at mealtimes. How prisons were "half-filled with black men. Black boys are five times as likely as white boys to be killed, four times as likely to be arrested, seven times as likely to be locked up, three times as likely to be suspended from school or drop out, four times as likely to be victims of violent crimes, and black teens commit 50% more violent crimes than whites — present company excepted." Richie could only shake his head and roll his eyes. He knew his father was right, but he didn't care to hear the mountain of facts and figures. He knew he was going to do something. Charles felt his son, like Lincoln, wanted to be remembered for making a contribution for something better.

Charles knew his son had identified more with being black than white. When he was yet a year or so from being of school age, he had asked Darlene if he could be white like her. Though lighter in complexion than his dark-skinned father, he was identified as a "black" child. Darlene had been upset at her boy's innocent question. That was when she decided they would move out of their white middle class neighborhood into the Shaw district, which had a large established black population with black churches, barbershops, and soul food restaurants.

Moving was not an easy decision, but Charles agreed with

Darlene. They wanted their son to be comfortable with that side of his culture. They wanted him to be around his people, to know it was okay to be black, and that it wasn't just Martin Luther King, Malcolm X, and Frederick Douglass that had been important in black history. Darlene wanted her son to be informed and active like she was as a young energetic teenager. When she went to parents' night at her son's school, there was at first the little surprise: "Oh, she's white."

Darlene was never shy about expressing who she was, and when she overheard one of her son's classmates ask, "Your mother's white?" she would warmly smile and say, "Yes, she is."

"And she would not tolerate someone treating our son in an unkind way. Darlene was always a mother protecting her cub."

Richie had come along well into Charles' and Darlene's marriage and was all the more welcomed. Evolution, thought Charles, could not have produced a more remarkable offspring. Richie had safely and academically navigated high school. He seemed to have a grasp of who he was; and while he was enamored of hip-hop and rap and ball caps, he had managed along the way to dodge whatever slings and arrows came his way.

Richie had thought a lot about his mixed-race. He had been researching his senior paper on slavery when he read about the Harvard professor during Lincoln's time who had maintained that blacks and mullatos were inferior and should not be assimilated into this country. Inferiority, Charles thought, had nothing to do with Richie's being on the losing end in a far-off country struggling for existence, and inferiority had nothing to do with Charles' father's lost battle for survival. But where Charles' father had little confidence, Charles' son had been brimming with confidence. Or had he? Charles wondered. Had slavery affected him, too? Despite

Richie's seeming self-assurance, maybe there was a residue of doubt. Despite Richie's doing well in school with the promise of college ahead, did he still see his options as limited? Maybe Richie thought the only place he could really blend in was the military.

Perhaps if the founders had truly committed to freeing the slaves, Charles himself wouldn't have felt the urgent need as a young man to be a hero. Maybe he would have been satisfied with being the fine young man his mother said he was. But as he told Darlene, "Though I didn't have a choice, I wanted to enlist. Our son has a choice." Perhaps Richie had not seen the choice so clearly.

FIFTEEN

Charles and Lincoln stood outside a boarded up old building, long ready for the wrecking ball. The dilapidated structure looked a little forbidding, as though it had been the setting of a sad story. It was where Charles grew up as a teenager. For a moment the building seemed to change in front of him as his memory took him back. The grass turned green, the paint on the wall smoothed into a fresh new coat. The boards disappeared, and the building looked as it did in 1961. Charles could see his mother standing in the doorway holding his ten-year-old hand. He could see his father turn away and walk down the sidewalk and out of his life with a suitcase in hand.

"Getting a job's easy," his daddy'd say. "It's keeping them that's hard."

The building now looked like what it was, an abandoned building with no sign of life. He walked up and pushed at the front door which was ajar. He and Lincoln went in. The rooms were gutted and empty. Charles walked toward a door at the end of a hallway. "This is the entrance to the apartment where my older brother Terry and my mother and I lived. The last time I was in this apartment was the night before I left for boot camp. It was the best day of my life up till then."

Charles was remembering that outside the apartment door there were always several pairs of shoes, when he thought he heard noise from inside. Charles started to remove his shoes. "Mother's golden rule." Lincoln leaned against the wall and began to remove his shoes — the Air Jordans.

"Look alive, Lincoln, there's a party going on."

Charles stood beside Lincoln as they watched the party unfold. There was live music. The saxophone player reminded Charles of the Musician he saw every day on the Mall. His mother Viola was posing for a picture with her two boys, Terry, 27, and Charles at 19 — Private Huggins, in his military dress uniform. Friends stood around talking excitedly about the future. Terry raised a glass in toast to the private. "My baby brother's going to be the black Abraham Lincoln." Lincoln gave a look to Charles. "He's going to save the world and make us all safe from Communism." Everybody at the party laughed.

Charles told Lincoln he had believed what his brother said all those years ago with all his might. "I was gung-ho."

"The beliefs of a child are often the most true things we ever know," said Lincoln.

It had been a heady time. Charles really felt if the world was not his oyster, then certainly his country was his for the asking. "Lord, what fools these mortals be," said Charles. "Everyone thought I was nuts, but I loved that uniform," he said, watching his younger self. "I was stupid. I didn't know zip."

"Where's Vietnam, Spit and Shine?" One of Terry's friends

razzed young Charles.

"He don't know where it is," said Terry. "There's a war going on right here, and my little brother wants to go clear across the world to fight." Vietnam was on another planet for all Charles knew at the time. Terry told everyone that his little brother wanted to be a hero. "Been watching John Wayne in *Sands of Iwo Jima* one too many times." The whole party again erupted in raucous laughter.

Charles could recall the many times he begged his brother to go with him to the latest John Wayne movie. He saw them all.

"Haven't you noticed that big, bad Duke is white?" Someone yelled. Young soldier Charles got his back up, "Courage has got nothing to do with color."

"Who said anything about courage. This is the draft." The laughter flowed.

"So you're not going?" young Charles asked, as though surprised.

"Uncle Sam can't run fast as I can," came the reply followed by another burst of laughter.

"Yeah," chimed in another.

"The draft's nothing but a poverty program," came another voice.

"Don't pay them any attention, Charles," his mother whispered.

Lincoln wanted to know about John Wayne.

"He was brave, strong, courageous, invincible, full of guts and glory — a crusader for justice."

"Sounds like a good soldier," said Lincoln.

"He looked good in a uniform."

"So did McClellan."

While Charles was in Vietnam, he had become disillusioned with Wayne. "Wayne wasn't real. Cardboard, an empty bill of goods."

"Sounds like McClellan. Wayne must've been a general," said Lincoln.

"Actor." Charles let the word out as if he'd taken a bite of something bitter.

"Good one?"

"Better than John Wilkes."

"That's not saying much. His brother Edwin was the actor."

"I know you were fond of Edwin. He loved Shakespeare like you and me. John Wilkes was jealous of Edwin. He didn't know 'jack' about Shakespeare or he wouldn't have been such a coward. Like Wayne, I thought I was a hero. Nice uniform. Real butch. Looked good, didn't I?"

Lincoln agreed that he did.

Charles and Lincoln watched while Terry held court at the party. He had always taken his role as big brother seriously, and it bothered him that his little brother was going to fight a war he disagreed with, but Terry loved his brother.

"My little brother's going to save the world over there, and I'll save it over here."

Terry had finished his community college degree and was an up-and-coming leader in his African-American neighborhood. In those days, you were forced to take sides.

"Terry knew which side he was on," said Charles.

"Town named Hadley, South Carolina," Terry's voice raised, "has the idea if you're black and an unregistered voter, you oughta stay that way. My old man was never allowed to vote," said Terry disdainfully. "He was afraid of the police. He was always second-class, always inferior, always distrustful, and always hopeless, never equal. We're going to introduce those virtuous white folks to a little thing called the Bill of Rights. It's about time this country lives up to what it says it is. We all have to make sure it does because no one else is going to. We have to educate the white man."

Everyone at the party cheered Terry's impassioned statement. Somebody said he should run for office.

"Foolish dreams ran in the family," said Charles. "My brother hated what Daddy went through. I think Terry was ashamed. He seethed with anger, was quick to attack what he saw as a wrong. He minced no words. He was tired of waiting for the government to take care of things. He felt we had stagnated; we were weighted down in apathy."

It was supposed to be a bloodless revolution. One young man hotly said that "losing blood was the only way to get the white man's attention. It's time we started kicking some cracker ass."

"Don't be a fool," said Terry.

"Fighting for what's right is not foolish."

"Losing your life is."

"Nobody's going to hurt me. We're going to bring some heat and make 'em sorry. I'm tired of peaceful protesting and getting shined on. Marching's not what we need. They hurt us, we hurt them."

"I'm against outright war because of the superior strength of the white majority. We can't do much good in jail and leaving the country is giving up," Terry warned.

"This is my son's party. You all stop your talking!" Charles' mother had put her foot down.

Charles recalled the bitter struggle of that time, still feeling Reverend King's leadership of non-violent protesting was the reason King and Terry had been successful. "My brother made a difference. I believe he accomplished more by his non-violence than I did in combat in Vietnam. That war only accentuated the legacy of racism that had ruled our daddy's life. My brother helped do what your war couldn't do. I don't mean that his sit-ins and marching took us to the promised land any more than your war did, but he did as much. It's just that no one knows or cares. It was a black thing."

Charles watched himself as the young soldier.

"That much fuss hadn't been made over me since I was May King. It was like a Sunday picnic."

Another woman about the same age as Charles' mother walked up to him at the party and gave him a little book of the complete works of Shakespeare "to take with you on your travels."

"She was my high school English teacher," Charles told Lincoln as they watched her give his younger self a hug. "Her personal mission had been to teach me Shakespeare. She read aloud as many of Shakespeare's plays to me and my classmates as she could. She had us act out scenes in her English class. She took a few of us around to places giving programs of memorized speeches from Shakespeare."

"She did a fine job of teaching," said Lincoln.

"Look, I asked Mama if she was proud of me."

"That's a silly question. Of course I'm proud. You're a smart boy. Just don't be too smart. You listen to your fear because sometimes it's telling you to not be so cocky. Don't worry, you got as much chance getting yourself killed right here as you do in China."

"Vietnam, Mama," laughed Charles.

"All I know is you'll be gone." Then she hugged him for the longest time. She could not let go.

"I was a mama's boy," Charles told Lincoln.

Young soldier Charles pulled away from his mother and promised her that he would return. She laid her hand on her son's face. "Keep to the rhythm son, keep to the rhythm and you won't get lost. Remember that, child."

So that he wouldn't forget, she embroidered those words on a piece of material she had slipped into his duffel bag. His Vietnam buddy, Willie from Philly, had spied Charles' mother's little homily under Charles' pillow at boot camp. One day when the company was on a training march, the drill sergeant blared out, "Keep to the rhythm, Huggins, and you won't get lost!" It seemed like the whole company was in on the joke. It was one of the rare light moments of the camp.

At the party, Charles and Lincoln saw a young girl walk up to the young handsome soldier. She was white, the only white person at young Charles' going away party. The beautiful girl would become Charles' wife. She worked as a volunteer at the community center his brother headed up. It was a storefront office that bustled with activist activity. Darlene was one of several young white students captivated by the stirring speeches of Martin Luther King.

"At first Terry did not welcome my blond, blue-eyed Darlene, but she would not be put off. Terry could not deny her spunky persistence, determination, and passion."

"Sounds like we both are acquainted with strong-willed women," Lincoln joked. "My Mary has a mind of her own."

After several months of working at the community center, Darlene was introduced to Charles. It was Terry who made the introduction.

"I started hanging around the community center after meeting her," said Charles. "In fact I started working there after school and on Saturdays. Terry was a demanding boss, but it was also a lot of fun. They formed committees, gathered court transcripts, helped distribute reports. It was a heady, insane, idealized time for a new generation. We were convinced we were going to change the world. It was just that Terry and I each had our own way of doing it.

"Darlene and I were very shy about our being seen together too much at first, and it was months before anyone truly guessed there was more than just friendship between us. In time though, rumors began to fly. Terry became concerned about the ramifications for his little brother if word got out that he was dating a white girl — especially during the civil rights and black nationalist time. At first Terry had wanted to fire Darlene from the community center, but I pleaded with him not to. After Darlene took me to her home to meet her parents, Terry became a convert to the relationship. He knew she really cared for me."

Darlene was quite taken with the charming young athlete and became quite brazen with her affections for him. Soon she was walking hand in hand with him down the street in her all-white neighborhood.

"That was a scene the neighbors had never seen before. She dared me to hold her hand the first time we went to her parents' house. It was innocent but . . . there was a high current of electricity flowing between us. More than I remember being in the Sidney Poitier movie, *Guess Who's Coming to Dinner*. Poitier's a black actor, debonair like Frederick Douglass," Charles told Lincoln. "What I really wanted to be when I grew up was Sidney Poitier, a trail blazer. Not an inferior bone in his body."

"Like Frederick Douglass," said Lincoln.

"Yeah, but white people love Poitier, the characters he played, charm with a capital 'C'. He was a hero, an actor — a good actor. So what if white people liked him — he was a trail blazer. Now I was no Poitier, no charmer, just a black kid from a black neighborhood but Darlene's parents were wonderful and I appreciated it.

"People would literally race to their windows to watch us walk by on her parents' street. Darlene's mother and father were concerned for her safety, but they were supportive of her. That made it easier for me."

"Occasionally, Darlene would hear a derisive comment hurled her way, but she ignored it. Those who didn't approve simply avoided her after it became known she had a black boyfriend. It didn't seem to matter to her one iota, but only deepened her feelings for the man she came to love and respect. For hours we would talk about our hopes and dreams.

"When I didn't receive the scholarship offer I wanted, I enlisted in the military. Darlene was furious, but she understood, and she told me she would be there when I returned."

"And she must have been."

◆　◆　◆

Darlene, it appeared to Lincoln, was quite comfortable in her surroundings at the party. Lincoln could see the strength in the assured way she conducted herself. He watched the young, pretty blond, wearing a long flowered dress that touched her ankles, as she approached the young Charles.

"You got a look to you, soldier boy."

"I do?" He had a full out ear-to-ear grin.

"Like nothing scares you."

"What do I have to be scared of?" His innocence and openness were irresistible to her.

"Dying in some far-off land."

"I don't plan on doing that. You see, I got to come back."

"Why's that?"

"I got too much to do here."

"What do you want to do?"

"Like you, I want to change the world. I'm just starting on the other side, that's all. Besides there's the dancing."

"The dancing?"

"Oh yes," said young Charles. "The dancing. Why don't we get started on that right now."

"Maybe it's too hot for dancing," she teased.

"Darlene, I'm about to go off and fight for this country. Unless I miss my guess, you're a part of it. Army manual says you should show your gratitude."

"Just because I'm grateful means I've got to dance with you?"

"No, but I'm hoping this does." Charles pulled a small box from his pocket. Darlene looked at him for a moment.

"Well, open it," said Charles impatiently.

She did. It was the ring she had hoped for and suspected was coming. Charles knew, as young as they were, this girl was for him. She had such a strong personality. He knew there was no way she would walk behind him. She would walk beside or a step in front, but never behind. And he was up to the challenge. He also knew she loved him.

"I'll dance with you, Marine, because I'll be supporting my future husband."

"Give me something nice to remember when things get rough."

"You'll need some good memories to march on."

"Your country thanks you, Miss."

"I was putty in her presence," Charles told Lincoln.

"Oh yes," Lincoln nodded.

"How'd you ever find anyone hard-headed enough to marry you?" Charles asked Lincoln.

"It was a profound wonder," laughed Lincoln.

Charles' expression was strained as he watched the young

dancers, his eyes sad. It had been a long time since he danced. He told Lincoln that he guessed he'd lost his rhythm. They walked back to the door and put on their shoes.

"You dance, Lincoln?" Charles asked.

Lincoln laughed and shook his head. "Not with these flat feet."

"You got your dancing shoes on."

Lincoln looked at the Air Jordans and smiled. "I like dancing. Mary loves to dance. Once I was dancing with my wife-to-be," he related. "Told her I'd wanted to dance with her in the worst way. 'Mr. Lincoln,' she said, 'you are dancing with me in the worst way.'"

Lincoln thought he could see the slightest of smiles creep across Charles' face. They watched back through the open door and across time as young Charles and Darlene spun around and around, lost in the moment. Lincoln commented on her beauty. Charles remembered how much he loved her then and how much he still loved her.

SIXTEEN

Charles and Lincoln walked through the Fort Dix Training Camp where both he and Richie had gone through basic training. Lincoln was interested in the fortified structure.

"This is one of the most fortified cities in the world."

"It's soon to be that way again."

Charles talked about his time as a young recruit traveling on a bus to boot camp. "I was excited and ready for anything — I thought. All the boys on the bus were black except for two white boys sitting together in a row behind me. Someone asked the white boys how come they were on the bus. 'Guess they ran out of blacks' came the answer. There was a big silence for a moment, but I couldn't help laughing. Before you knew it, the whole bus was laughing, including the two white boys.

"We all stopped laughing, though, after a week in camp dressed in fatigues lined up facing a row of attack dummies hanging from a wooden platform. We all carried rifles with bayonets attached, and the drill sergeant was always screaming in our ears. 'You will thrust, you will jab, you will kill. You will kill and kill again.' "

Charles' boy had learned bayonet fighting, too. The marines had toughened up their hand-to-hand combat training since the Vietnam War. Charles saw Richie in uniform, bayonet in hand.

"Spring forward," commanded the drill sergeant. "Don't hop! If you do not spring forward, you will die."

"You would have been in trouble, Lincoln, the way you walk."

"I was a pretty good jumper — though not in a league with Mr. Jordan," said Lincoln, recalling the poster he had seen earlier in the Nike store window.

"I remember my drill sergeant asking what I thought was the purpose of having a bayonet."

"Sir, to stick my enemy as quickly and as many times as freaking possible, sir!"

"That is correct, soldier!"

"A good bayonet is indispensable. Your life could depend upon it," said Lincoln, a student of weapons. He had tested some of them on the White House lawn.

"Told us they would teach us a skill. Guess killing was easier to teach than reading and writing."

Charles could still hear his drill sergeant's voice cutting through the pages of time as green-fatigued recruits, among them his Richie, in the middle of a simulated jungle, attacked dummies hanging from a wooden platform.

"If it moves, what do we do?" the drill sergeant bellowed.

"We kill it," the recruits yelled.

"If it is not Marine green, what do we do?"

"We kill it. We kill everything! We kill dogs, cats, chickens, cows, women, children — we are death itself."

As he and Lincoln watched, Charles was dumbstruck by the total commitment to killing. "My God. Killing or being killed seems, in the heat of battle, to make perfect sense."

"Perhaps the only thing that does make sense at those times," said Lincoln.

"Home and family didn't seem as real as the fight," recalled Charles — his voice distant.

"I never knew the heat of battle. I only saw the horror," said Lincoln

"You will kill or be killed!" The sergeant's jarring statement of fact quieted the recruits. "Do you understand that, you pathetic bunch of momma's boys?"

"Yes sir!"

"You may very well find yourselves in an Afghan cave where your bayonet is going to be your best friend. We will make you or break you! Or both! Do you hear me?"

"Yes sir!" It was Richie's baby face contorting into a fierceness that Charles did not recognize. Richie pouncing on the attack dummy with a bloodcurdling scream, slashing it again and again. "Thrust! Jab! Kill! Thrust! Jab! Kill! Kill! Kill!"

"Spring forward, don't hop. If you do not, you will die. Again!" The drill sergeant had stopped Richie.

"I'm talking to you Huggins!"

Richie plowed forward again, slashing into the dummy with a bloodcurdling yell.

"Make sure he is dead," barked the drill sergeant.

Richie screamed and stabbed the dummy in the heart. Charles could barely catch his breath at seeing his soldier son. "What was I so sure of? So ready to kill for?" Charles' knees felt weak, and he sat on a nearby bench. "I was gung-ho all right, John Wayne.

Wanted to be a hero — serve my country."

Charles recalled for Lincoln a flight to Vietnam he took with a planeload of other green soldiers. The stewardess served them drinks. Private Huggins was living first class. He knew what his mission was. He grinned, taking a sip of his first whiskey. Then he got off the plane. Lincoln stood beside Charles on the tarmac as they watched young Huggins in uniform come down the stairs from the plane, which had landed at a bustling Army airstrip. US soldiers milled about waiting to board the plane. These soldiers had a much different expression than the young, ignorant fresh-faced Huggins.

Charles remembered having made eye contact with one of those soldiers whose arm was in a sling. The soldier stared a little vacantly and handed the new replacement a small statue of the Virgin Mary. "Welcome to Disneyland. You Catholic?"

"No," answered young Huggins.

"Doesn't matter. She won't mind. She'll look out for you. She got me out of here alive."

Young Charles asked how the soldier knew it was the Virgin Mary that got him out.

"Faith, brother. It's all about faith. Lose that and your goose is cooked."

With that the soldier climbed into the plane, the first leg of his journey home. Huggins looked at the statue for a second before shoving it into his pocket.

Charles observed, "I thought it was funny at the time, but there wasn't much funny after that. Soon I wanted to run like the wind, but contrary to what you wish, we don't all get to run the same race."

"All must have an unfettered start in the race of life," said Lincoln.

"That lifts my heart, Jezebel. Repeating it doesn't make it true."

"But if you say it enough, perhaps it will be true," Lincoln said.

145

Lincoln was surprised by the number of black soldiers, then he remembered the photo he'd seen in Charles' apartment of several young black soldiers.

"Find it hard to believe?" Charles asked. "Believe it or not, we can lock and load and talk at the same time. Some of us can even quote Shakespeare."

They watched as young Huggins cleaned his rifle. His clothes were sweat-stained, and he still looked very raw. There was a veteran soldier next to him, playing a harmonica.

Willie from Philly gave them a little riff on his harmonica. Willie had no regard for any cause. He never met an order he felt wasn't stupid, but he carried out those orders without regard for his own life. He wore sunglasses all the time and smoked all the time, usually in combat — except at night. At night he had to cool it with the cigarettes because the Cong might see the glow from the lit cigarette. He wore a tie-dyed shirt under his army vest.

"I couldn't understand how he could feel the way he did — like he didn't have faith in anything. I now know how he felt. Whenever Willie was upset or just wanted to think about nothing, he would pull out his harmonica. I went to sleep many times listening to his music."

Lincoln nodded.

"Whenever I would say something about serving my country, Willie couldn't stop laughing."

"Say what?" he'd say.

"Serve my country."

Willie laughed even harder.

"There's nothing funny about it."

Willie would do a number on me for the company."

"Don't feed me no humble pie Messa Lincoln, bless de Lord, is cum at las' to free his children from bondage. Glory hallelujah! Our savior, the Great Emancipator. My ass! The only reason honest Abe didn't own slaves is because he couldn't afford them. But Uncle Sam can. We're just property, expendable property. What'r you doing over here? You better get back on that plane. Go back and clean up after your cherry tree-chopping friend, Honest Abe."

"That was Washington, you fool. Everyone would laugh," Charles explained, "and that would inspire Willie to even greater heights at my expense. But I held my own, telling him it was a privilege to fight for democracy. And that you, Lincoln, had freed the slaves so people like him could make a fool of himself. Willie said he couldn't believe I was black."

"I heard some fool talking, but you go to the head of the line," said Willie.

"Fighting for what's right isn't foolish."

"You keep spouting that nonsense and you ain't gonna make it another two months 'in country.' Listen to Willie from Philly. You learn fast in war. You better. Now, I can bend and bow with the best of them. You roll out that 'serve my country' crap 'cause a three hundred year-old habit's hard to break. We're just bodies, you know. Population control. We're the new poverty program. That's it. You see what I'm saying? The country's been built; all the cotton's picked. We ain't got no country. You think Uncle Sam gives a good shit about your sorry ass? It's all bull-shit. We're over here killing people because they don't live the way we want them to live. It's almost funny."

I had no comeback.

◆ ◆ ◆

Charles and Lincoln watched the chastised young private as he slowly got up and walked away from his fellow Marines.

"I was a greenhorn," said Charles. "Willie took it upon himself to get me back home alive. He was the bravest soldier I ever knew."

SEVENTEEN

As they walked back across the Mall in front of Lincoln's Memorial, Charles looked at his image in the reflecting pool. Fireworks were still booming. Lincoln's eyes lit up, but Charles didn't seem to notice. Lincoln asked Charles if he could hear them.

"I'm not deaf, just a lot of noise."

"The annual joyous return of equality," Lincoln beamed.

"The carnival comes once a year," muttered Charles.

"America's birthday," countered Lincoln. "How long since the first time in the history of the world a nation by its representatives, assembled and declared as a self-evident truth that all men are created equal. How long? How long?"

"Who cares, who cares," came the dry response from Charles as he walked on. Lincoln frowned at Charles' attitude.

"The annual joyous return of equality. It is good news!"

"Real heartwarming," said Charles.

Their attention was directed across the street where, as if he could hear their banter, the Musician was wailing, *Ain't That Good News*. While holding an extended note with one hand, he retrieved from his pocket shredded pieces of colored confetti with the other and threw them into the air. A couple of homeless men had joined the Musician's celebration, making their own confetti by shredding the newspapers they had been lying on.

Lincoln and Charles watched as the fireworks climaxed, spewing bright colors through the still languid night air. Then it was quiet, and the Musician wove his musical magic with the spiritual *Over My Head*.

Lincoln and Charles were entranced by the sounds of the lonely saxophone. It seemed as close to any religious experience as Lincoln had ever had. Later as they dodged the traffic and people who had come to the Mall to see all the festivities and were now trying to be the first ones home, Lincoln said the celebration was a reminder that all men are created equal. Charles wasn't impressed.

Charles and Lincoln both knew America was a tough place to be poor. They had both watched their fathers always moving, never able to stop long enough in one place to truly belong.

Charles said, "There is the illusion of equality, but there's only so much room at the top in this country."

"That may be," Lincoln said, "but my ancient faith taught me that all men are created equal."

"Unequal is unequal. Why do some folks get silver spoons, and some get lumps of dirt?"

"Poverty is not necessarily a reason for unhappiness or struggle."

Charles rolled on, "Why do some have health care, and some don't? Why are some sharp, and some aren't too swift? Why do some get good teachers, and some get slimebags? Why do some have books, and some can't read? Why do some have family, and some grow up on the streets? Why do some have luck, and some don't? Some kids even have a daddy for president. Some don't."

Lincoln seemed greatly bothered by what Charles had said. He wanted to discuss this more. "Why don't you come over to the shop? We can sit around or maybe go over to Seward's house and talk." The "shop" was how Lincoln often referred to his office on the second floor of the White House.

"I thought it was only a rumor that you still lived at the White House. As much as your name is bandied about today, I figured you had your old room back."

Lincoln was pleased to see some humor from Charles.

"Why do you want to talk with me? I don't sing, don't dance anymore, and I'm not funny—" Charles murmured.

"I'll tell the jokes."

"Try to restrain yourself," pleaded Charles.

"I have a few good stories," said Lincoln.

Charles shook his head and walked on.

Lincoln strode to his side. "I want to know, Charles, about the current state of affairs in Washington.

"Then I'll start with a question. Do you know what the black man's burden is?"

"I'd like to hear it from you."

"Educating white folks. My brother said that was the black man's burden."

"Then I think it's necessary for us to talk. If I just speak with other white people, what will I learn?"

"Aren't we wrapped up in each other's hopes and dreams?"

"And beds," Charles knowingly added. "Your friend Jefferson planted a few seeds and not all of them were in his garden."

Lincoln voiced no opinion of Jefferson, but he did chuckle,

conceding that he had heard rumors about Jefferson but never spent much time thinking about it. "I know, though, he was a Renaissance man."

"Certain things I guess we don't need to talk about," Charles mused, asking Lincoln, "Are you willing to eat what I cook?"

"Reminds me of an old acquaintance who, having a son of a scientific turn, bought him a microscope. The boy went around, experimenting with his glass upon everything. One day, at the dinner-table, his father took up a piece of cheese. 'Don't eat that, Father,' said the boy, 'it is full of wrigglers.' 'My son,' replied the old gentleman, taking a huge bite, 'let 'em wriggle; I can stand it if they can.'"

Charles said that some people just can't help talking about things they know nothing about.

Lincoln acknowledged that speaking out of ignorance was a dangerous thing in his profession. "About the only way to avoid that is to say nothing at all."

Charles nodded. "Talking nonsense is a pretty common trait among politicians."

"I would have to agree with that, Mr. Huggins."

"Well, you're not totally ignorant, then," Charles responded.

"Thank you for the small compliment."

"You're welcome," replied Charles.

EIGHTEEN

"The struggle of today's not altogether for today. It's for a vast future also," said Lincoln.

"Whose future would that be?" Charles asked.

"Everyone's," Lincoln replied.

Just then gunshots echoed in the next block. For a moment they thought it might be rogue fireworks, but police sirens began wailing, and two police cars sped quickly by.

"There's the future," Charles said.

"That's war," observed Lincoln.

"That's D.C."

With that, another police car zoomed past them with lights flashing and siren blaring. Lincoln surveyed the scene. "At what point should we expect the approach of danger?"

"When you see a black man," Charles said dryly, feeling somewhat guilty for having the thought in his mind.

"The complaints I hear of thee are grievous," Lincoln responded, quoting Shakespeare.

A challenge was laid out once again. Charles fielded it cleanly. "S' blood, my Lord, they are false."

"Swearest thou, ungracious boy?"

Charles paused before responding as they watched the patrol car come to a halt behind the two other police cars at the nearby intersection. Several black men were standing in front of a corner store, drinking and smoking. They laughed as the police pulled up. One young man started yelling at the officers. The police got out of their patrol cars. This was the kind of scene Charles and Darlene had worked hard to make sure their son was not attracted to. Gangs, racial tensions with police, popular culture were land mines that affected all young black men. Charles tossed another quote Lincoln's way: "Wherein is he good, but to taste sack and drink it?"

Lincoln returned: "Wherein neat and cleanly, but to carve a capon and eat it?"

Charles and Lincoln stood watching the police confront the men while continuing their sparring of quotes with Charles holding forth: "Wherein cunning but in craft, wherein crafty but in villainy? Wherein villainous, but in all things?"

And in unison they said, "Wherein worthy but in nothing?"

The lead officer called out, "Let's break up the party, boys."

"We're just celebratin' America's birthday, officer."

Then another young man held out a beer bottle. "You want some of our champagne?"

"No, thanks," the officer said, as three other officers lined the men up against a wall and patted them down looking for weapons.

"You fear the black man, he fears you, and you both run from spiders. Same fear," said a concerned Lincoln, his brow furrowed.

154

There was some scuffling and loud protests as two officers had their guns drawn and held at their side while the other officers confiscated a couple of handguns.

"It's the same old, same old," Charles noted. "The men are strong, cocky, young, stupid, and for sale. And if no one's buying, the devil's offering."

It was easy for some, Charles felt, to dismiss the dangers that lurked because the dangers didn't seem apparent at first sight. People seemed to go and come, doing their chores, running their errands. Charles and Darlene had subtlety schooled their son on how to make it in the no-longer-quite-so-white but still *predominately* white world. The trick, they discovered, was to teach him about the changing subtleties of the black community. These were perhaps harder to navigate and certainly to converse about.

Charles knew it was a real powder keg for the young men on the corner, as if their feet were encased in the cement. "They got no hope 'cause they think this is as good as it's going to get," he told Lincoln. "Used to be these boys would run from the police."

"And now?" Lincoln asked.

Charles shook his head. "Half the time, they shoot at 'em. Like the wild west, crazy. They'd just as soon go down in a blaze of glory. It's a war. We may be the only unarmed people on this block at the moment."

A couple of the young men were handcuffed and led to a patrol car. Lincoln didn't know what to make of what he was seeing. Charles explained that it was a police raid on gang members, some of whom were probably violating parole.

Lincoln reminisced, "While in Congress I could look out the windows of the Capitol and see the Georgia pen, a Negro livery stable where droves of Negroes were collected, strung together like so many fish on a trot line, and then finally sent to southern markets, like droves of horses."

They watched as police loaded in the young men.

"Now *they're* on a prison line," Charles said as the police cars drove off.

"Bolted in with a lock of a hundred keys, the keys in the hands of a hundred different men, and then scattered to a hundred different and distant places," Lincoln added.

"It's like a giant maze. Hooked, booked, or dead."

"I've never seen a prison stop another killing," said Lincoln, wiping his brow with his handkerchief. "Like the man said about his mules, 'We're always looking at the ass end of things.' "

NINETEEN

Lincoln and Charles walked a long time in silence, Lincoln finally breaking the stillness. "It is my earnest desire to know the will of Providence, and if I can learn what it is, I will do it if at all possible."

Charles did not reply at once and then quoted a favorite line from *Macbeth*: "If you can look into the seeds of time, and say which grain will grow and which will not…"

Lincoln smiled picking the line right up: "Speak then to me."

"I must know if the sacrifices I asked were worth it." Lincoln said. "I know my words will be insufficient but I hope my energy will be such that it allows me to continue to learn about a world where sympathy is needed for all."

"I don't want your sympathy," Charles stated curtly.

Eventually they found themselves at the Jefferson Memorial. There were still a good many tourists despite the cumbersome security blockades. Lincoln read an informational plaque outside the

157

Memorial. Charles told Lincoln that the Jefferson Memorial wasn't as attractive for the birds as his Memorial because Jefferson's Memorial was more open. He pointed overhead.

"That's a stone dome, nothing else. There's no iron or steel in it. It's a real classical building. Maybe the last one built in this country. Fitting for an aristocrat like Jefferson."

"All honor to Jefferson," said Lincoln.

"The man ought to have a white sheet over his head instead of this stone dome," said Charles.

Lincoln looked incredulously at Charles. Then after a considered silence, he said, "History requires sifting the wheat from the chaff, but it is worth the effort. There is much to admire about Jefferson. He wrote the Declaration of Independence."

"Declaration's not worth the paper it's written on," Charles said as he moved on. This pronouncement was too much even for Lincoln's calm demeanor.

"The Declaration was written on the toils that were endured by the officers and soldiers of the army who achieved independence and on the backs of those who adopted the Declaration so that all should have an equal chance, including you."

"I'm going to put you back in your highchair."

Lincoln responded, "I was deeply moved when I stood there in the place where there was so much wisdom, and patriotism, and devotion to principle from which sprang the institutions under which we live."

Charles took a beat shaking his head and laughing.

"What's so funny?" Lincoln asked.

"You're tenacious."

"No, I'm just slow to learn and slow to forget what I've learned."

"Then you must remember that Jefferson traded slaves, lots of them. He was against whites and blacks marrying, and like you, he wanted to ship us out of the country."

Lincoln was silent as they walked on, ending up at the Washington Monument, the bottom third of which, Lincoln said, was built during the Civil War. Again there were a great number of tourists. The grounds had recently been renovated due to new security measures. They stood looking up at the tall Monument while in the midst of their continuing discussion. Lincoln said, "Washington fought for more than independence."

"Really," Charles replied. "What exactly did he fight for? The right to own more slaves?"

With that he unlocked the door to the Monument, and they went inside. They climbed the stairs, Charles leading the way. Their discussion continued as they made their way to the top.

"Washington was pretty near perfect," said Lincoln, "and was someone we could all aspire to."

"Speak for yourself."

"He fought for a promise that the weight should be lifted from the shoulders of all men and that all should have an equal chance."

Charles was tired of hearing about "equal." He increased his pace up the stairs. Lincoln, despite his Air Jordans, had to talk to Charles' back. "Washington was the one who mattered. He was a hero. The unity of this nation was of paramount importance to him. He understood the stakes for the future. Without him there would have been no country."

Charles was now taking the steps two at a time. There was a time Lincoln would have taken the steps two at a time, but he was not in the best of shape, and he struggled as they neared the top. Charles reached the last step and turned around and looked down to see Lincoln breathing hard but making his way up.

"You remember your 'house divided' speech?" asked Charles.

"I do," panted Lincoln.

Charles quoted a little of the speech: ". . . a house divided against itself can't stand . . . this government can't survive half slave and half free."

Lincoln struggled to catch his breath and climb the last few steps. He paused filling his lungs. "I know the speech. I spent some time writing it."

" '. . .it'll become all one thing or all the other.' "

"That was a prediction only," Lincoln said, puffing as he reached the top. He laid his old boots down as he walked over to the edge of the monument.

"That was a good prediction. Came true, as you wanted. Became all white."

Again, Lincoln did not respond.

From the top of the Washington Monument, a refreshed Charles and a still panting Lincoln enjoyed the view. Lincoln was taken with how beautiful the capital was at night with all the buildings lit up. He was a city boy at heart. "I like cities. I felt at home in Chicago."

He was pleased with how vibrant Washington looked. He recalled his first inaugural and how regrettably he had to leave the party that night to deal with Fort Sumter. "That time was most strenuous. The capital was an open door, came close to losing it."

Lincoln said at first he didn't believe the South would go to war. He didn't believe they would secede over the issue of slavery. "Secession was against the Constitution. After many states seceded, many southerners didn't feel succession would lead to war. But when it did, the South was convinced of victory."

"Guess you and the South were both wrong," said Charles.

Lincoln explained that he always felt we were all Americans despite our differences.

"Unfortunately, not everyone feels that way," responded Charles.

"We have paid a severe price in human life to keep this nation together," Lincoln said looking out over the Capital. "Force and regrettably violence are sometimes needed to ensure the principle of one nation — one people. Good must be stronger than evil. That is why I wrote that 'house divided' speech."

"A newspaper account of that speech sold for $500,000."

"Nonsense," replied Lincoln, utterly disbelieving.

"It's true. It had been taken from one of Lincoln's scrapbooks for the Lincoln - Douglas debates. One of your relatives had it framed and it was hanging on a wall."

Lincoln could not comprehend that one of his speeches could have possibly sold for that kind of money. Charles was enjoying Lincoln's amazement. "You wouldn't happen to know where any more of your words are hanging around?"

Lincoln was disturbed. "May their devilish heads be shot off." He removed his hat but not before slapping his hand hard against the overlook. He rubbed his forehead. "Is that what it's all about, money?"

"What do you think?"

Lincoln looked at Charles for a moment and regrettably knew the answer. They both stared out at the night. They looked toward the Capitol with the Statue of Freedom at the top looking back. Charles thought he could see the Musician pushing his cart far below. The statue, Charles told Lincoln, was put there with the help of freed slaves.

"Yes. I insisted the work on the Capitol continue during the war."

David L. Selby

"I told my son the statue atop the dome was called Freedom."

Freedom for whom? Richie had wanted to know.

"Those slaves must have had heavy hearts of irony putting up a statue to freedom when they, themselves, had been slaves," said Charles.

Lincoln nodded.

Charles had wanted his son to know about slavery, about its place in America's flawed history. "Slavery probably killed more people than the Holocaust," he had told his son, "and it lasted a whole lot longer."

Some people still didn't get it. He recalled the story that he had read in the paper about the prosecutor who walked into a courtroom to try a murder case with a noose swinging from his chest! The prosecutor said the noose was just a joke. Some joke," Charles fumed to Lincoln. Darlene had cut the article out of the paper and attached it to their refrigerator.

It was a similar article that Alice, his fellow Memorial worker, had told him about earlier that day where a couple of lawyers walked into a Louisiana courtroom wearing ties with little nooses imprinted on them. "The lawyers were stupid for wearing the racist ties, but at least they were out front with it. It was probably more a case of stupidity than racism, but the perception that racism is alive and well was real. Truth is we got far greater problems — like education, and gangs, broken families, worse than racism, though many don't see it that way. The truth's hard, and not always fair."

It was the enemy you couldn't see that bothered ex-combat soldier Charles, where racist remarks are subtle and where there is a code of silence that prevents one from complaining because of fear of retaliation. Charles was used to the lawyers' kind of machismo humor and personally had always tried to stay above the fray. Now

162

his son was dead, for no good reason that he could discern, having been sent overseas to supposedly fight on America's behalf. And the latest headline read, "KKK to demonstrate at Antietam."

Before his son's death, Charles would have shrugged off this headline. Not any more.

TWENTY

"The African-American Civil War Monument is the only memorial to the Civil War's United States Colored Troops — all 208,000 who fought in the war. The memorial is not on the Mall but up here in the Shaw District not too far from my apartment. Darlene, Richie and I went to the dedication a few years ago. This monument was long overdue. It took the efforts of the whole African-American community many years to finally bring it to reality. Soldiers are sculpted into the front, and sculpted on the back are family members gathered around a departing soldier.

"Around the edge of the monument, you see the names of African-Americans who fought in the war — many of them have descendants living in this Shaw District. You won't see too many tourists up here looking at this monument, though," Charles noted.

He and Lincoln looked around. They were the only visitors on this evening of America's birthday.

"How many museums do you see on slavery in this town?

They're building one *out* of town, but *in* this town—zero. This is the capital. They got a big Indian museum down on the Mall. That place was a forest. It was the slaves who cut all the trees," Charles reminded Lincoln. "We got companies around here today made a ton of money from owning slaves."

Charles wiped the sweat from his face. He was not feeling well, wondering how many times he had covered the same territory, said the same things, played the same mind games of what he could have done better, differently.

"Frederick Douglass said you would be good soldiers," said Lincoln who was walking around admiring the monument.

"Despite my color. Good old obedient, patriotic, happy-go-lucky, solid as a wall, never flagging in devotion Charles. That was me. Stupid. We weren't all good soldiers, not all anything. If we were so good, why were you so slow in enlisting black troops? You were slower than Washington during the Revolution, and you needed us as much as he did."

Lincoln reflected back a moment, thinking about conversations he'd had with Frederick Douglass. "Moved as fast as I could. I couldn't risk the Border States' goodwill."

"You sure you weren't thinking that if a slave is good enough to be a soldier, then he can't be good to be a slave? I mean, you wouldn't call a soldier inferior, would you?"

Lincoln shook his head.

"That could have presented a bit of a problem, wouldn't you say? Wasn't it Douglass who told you men don't fight with one hand when they can fight with two?"

Lincoln nodded.

"What about paychecks?" Charles was beginning to pace around the Monument.

"Why were you so slow in getting us paychecks?" He felt a strong personal emotional tie to those slaves. His great-great grandfather had broken free of his masters and fought for the Union.

"They got their paychecks."

"Eventually," said Charles, "but the white soldier got thirteen dollars a month, the black soldier got seven dollars a month. And what about getting to vote?"

"I wanted it."

"You did?" Charles laughed, " 'Wanted it' doesn't mean squat."

"That's not what I meant," Lincoln protested.

"If you didn't mean it, what did you mean?"

"I meant nothing at all. It should be left up to each state. I don't push people where they don't want to go."

"What you mean is," Charles said, "that if we could have voted, some of us might have ended up in Congress. And you didn't want an inferior congressman. I believe you said "only the very intelligent black might be allowed to vote."

Lincoln lowered his head taking a long pause before saying, "I have gone along with the times."

"That's easy," said Charles shaking his head.

"Nobody thought too much about it," said Lincoln.

"You had a choice, Lincoln."

"At the time," Lincoln tried to explain, "I did not see such a choice in the offing."

"You weren't crazy about letting blacks be citizens. Blacks weren't allowed to cross state lines. No wonder my daddy felt out-of-place anywhere but the South. We call that racism today."

"You might say racism was rampant in my state of Illinois, as deep and long as the Mississippi."

"Yes," said Charles, "and you were one of them who wanted to keep blacks not only out of Illinois, but out of the entire western part of the country. Put a fence around it all."

Lincoln took a handkerchief from his hat and wiped his forehead. "A politician couldn't survive if he didn't put his finger to the public wind."

"You wanted to be elected," Charles said plainly, his face expressionless. "Were you a leader or a follower?"

"Just trying to keep things from getting worse," said Lincoln.

"So your solution was to ship us out of the country on the first boat."

"There had been an unwillingness among some whites, harsh as it may be, for you people to remain with us."

"Some whites included you."

"Yes . . . . I thought it would be better for both races to separate."

"Did you ever ask what we wanted to do?"

"Jefferson felt the same way."

"Well then, I guess that made it right. They shouldn't have brought us over in the first place."

"I agree," said Lincoln. "Your race suffered greatly living among us, and ours suffered from your presence."

"Even though most of this country was built on our backs."

The discussion was getting testy. "I didn't know about all the races in a single country. At the time I didn't know if we could live together."

Charles thought about that for a moment. "Didn't that strike you as being just a bit un-Christian?"

"The less talk about religion, the better," Lincoln replied. "I thought at the time it would be better to be separated. I felt your best chances of obtaining total equality were in another country."

"Some country where the weather was hot because everyone

knows we do much better in hot weather. Isn't that right?"

"Well, someplace that would be more suitable to your physical condition."

"You're a racist."

"But for your race among us, there would have been no war."

"Our race was not the cause of your war!" Charles took a strong affront to Lincoln's statement. "It was the unwillingness of your people to do us simple justice! Face it, white folks have had a hard time thinking of us as equals, and that goes for you, too." Charles was worked up. "Want to rub us out, do it proper-like, with guns, bows and arrows, sling shots, knives, drugs. But if you really want to rub us out, just continue to *not* teach our children to read and write."

Lincoln tried to calm him, but with a father's anguish Charles went on. "One thing I know is if blood is going to be shed, then the purpose must be worth while or there will be hell to pay. I assume the issue of slavery was worthwhile."

"If slavery's not wrong, nothing's wrong," said Lincoln. "Can't remember when I didn't so think and feel. I suppose when I was school age, I never thought much about it. No one I knew then was against it."

"I hear a sermon coming on."

"Slavery's a monstrous injustice."

Hearing this, Charles thought of his son's words about Lincoln being a dictator who did what he wanted. "So why didn't you just get up one morning and say, 'Doggonit, I'm gonna free the slaves today.'"

"When the time was right."

"When was it ever wrong?"

"Certainly before Kentucky and Maryland were in the fold."

"People still don't get it or don't want to get it. Act like they never heard of slavery, or they're ashamed or feel guilty. Slavery's the reason men were killing each other in the first place. Am I right? The fight was against slavery."

"Insurrection."

"The war was about slavery. Yes or no," demanded Charles.

"Yes."

"Thank you."

"The threatened spread of it gave me a cause," said Lincoln. "It was the bravery and commitment of the black soldier who convinced me otherwise about their being enlisted in the war. I would have been damned in time and eternity if I had returned to slavery those black warriors. The whole mess was regretful."

"People have been regretting ever since. Pain and shame, but they don't want to own up. They worry more about the shame than they do the people."

"I've never willingly planted a thorn in any man's bosom," said Lincoln.

"You didn't willingly announce emancipation either."

"I told you, when the time was right."

"And I asked you, when was it ever wrong?"

"If McClellan failed at Antietam, then any emancipation would have been fodder for my critics. They would have hailed it as a desperate act of a failed presidency. People would have laughed. Would my word free the slaves? No. Lee was on the march. Stopping him at Antietam and forcing him back into Virginia was an unexpected gift. I found religion. As it was, McClellan barely got out with any credibility. The North wouldn't support a war on slavery. A man watches his pear tree day after day, impatient for the ripening of the fruit. Let him attempt to force the process, and he may spoil both the fruit and tree."

"So what's another hundred years? You weren't going to do anything. You're a southern boy, Kentucky born, a segregationist at heart."

"I was not on the ballot of any southern state."

"You were too timid, Lincoln. That's what upsets me," said Charles.

"You may be right. A man cannot always do what he wants to do when he wants to do it. If that means people think you are a racist, so be it. But if I am to be remembered for anything, it should be for the Emancipation Proclamation. At the time my popularity was nil. I was very alone, but you go on. I learned a great deal. Frederick Douglass made me a better man. Emancipation was important for me. It was a new direction. Black soldiers enlisted and are vital — the biggest help up to that point of the rebellion. It has weakened the South. Slavery was critical to the Confederacy. I had a right to confiscate property in conquered territory. I refused to return slaves to their owners in Virginia because Virginia was in rebellion. I would not retract the Emancipation or modify it, nor would I return to slavery any person who was freed by its terms. I should be burned in hell, deservedly so, if things revert to the status quo."

"Emancipation was a by-product of your war," said Charles. "Besides, how free could the slaves be when you didn't even give them a piece of toilet paper to wipe their butts with?"

Lincoln had no immediate response, but his body seemed to take on a heavy load. He could only nod his head, finally saying, "It was not an easy time. I tried to study the facts, tried to correct errors when shown to be errors, determine what we knew about the other side, see what was possible, learn what was wise and right, and then act accordingly."

Charles' innocence had been battered in Vietnam, but with the help of his wife, he had nursed his lost innocence back to health. After Vietnam, Charles had groped around for a sense of identity, finding himself on the outside, not part of the elite, not welcomed, socially marginal like his father, he had thought. It was during this time that Charles acquainted himself with America's shrines. At first he could only walk for a short time with the aid of a cane, but gradually he and Darlene visited all the shrines. Their favorite walk was during spring and cherry blossom time. When they finally got a car, they took field trips to Washington's home at Mount Vernon and Jefferson's at Monticello. Charles couldn't pinpoint exactly why he had gotten interested in America's history, but he knew it had to do with his experience in Vietnam and with the struggle for civil rights for which his brother Terry had lost his life.

Charles' appetite for some meaning and self-worth in his life had led him, with the untimely death of his friend and fellow worker whose charge had been the Lincoln Memorial, to request reassignment to Lincoln and the Memorial. It was at the Memorial that Charles had found some satisfaction. A sense of justice was in the air, something his father had never felt.

Now weighted down with alienation and disenchantment, he sat on a wall that curved around the African-American Civil War Monument. He watched as Lincoln read aloud some of the names of the black Civil War soldiers. Charles saw the set of Lincoln's face etched in lines of pain, the haunting eyes, the heavy shoulders, and he could not help feeling empathy for the man.

TWENTY - ONE

The Capitol, lit for the celebration, loomed in the distance. Charles thought the glow had dimmed a little from problems so great that Lincoln's beloved Union could sink from the weight of them. Then what? Charles wondered. Would what Lincoln feared become a reality, that other countries would consider our form of government to be vulnerable?

The red, white, and blue banners were still. There was not the hint of a breeze, and the night seemed only a bit cooler to a weary Charles. His energy was being taxed further by Lincoln's long strides, causing Charles to take two steps to every one of his.

Charles watched a cat slowly cross the road ahead, indifferent about getting to the other side. The cat might be lucky, he thought. It had no notion of a past or future. He remembered again his father saying once you know something, nobody can take it away from you. That also had a down side. Charles knew he would be alone with his own history for the duration. Could he stand the weight of that history? He thought, if America could survive its recent history, there might be hope, but he told Lincoln that the chances of anyone being around in a hundred years was fifty-fifty.

The question was, could Charles understand his history and the country's history in a way that would allow him to move on. He could see his father and grandfather, see the struggle in their faces. He could see their faces in his. He would forever see his lost son's face. This was his destiny. Would he ever glimpse again the lost inner child, the dancer, the love buried deep within? Could he ever recapture the childhood innocence when he had no power or urge to harm. As a young soldier he had felt some kind of power, and he had learned to harm — to kill. Had that been true for his son, he wondered, in the quagmire of Iraq?

"We never learned a thing from Vietnam," he had lamented to Darlene. "It's a vicious cycle, and there's no end in sight."

Charles and Lincoln had made it up the hill and stood on the grass in front of the steps to the Capitol and the halls of Congress.

"All during this Civil War, the Capitol has been a barrack, a mess hall, and a medical office."

"I've read you had little use for Congress."

"I've had no choice. I've paid little heed to Congress during the war, especially in the beginning."

"You made generous use of executive power continuously throughout the war."

Lincoln did not respond. He was concentrating on the construction that was taking place around the Capitol.

"Admit it, you threw the Constitution out the window because it was in your way. You called the shots — no pun intended — all of them."

"I am . . . was the President."

173

"You made it easier for some to forget about certain laws, easier to just put the Constitution on the shelf for a day or two, easier to just look the other way when it suited them, and in the end made it easier for my son to be killed."

Charles looked at Lincoln for a response. Lincoln was somber. Charles knew he had struck a chord. The soldiers deaths clearly weighed heavily on Lincoln's shoulders.

"I thought I would be able to temper the situation. I overestimated my abilities. Some southerners felt that secession would not bring war — but my motive was clear, and that was to preserve the Union."

"Yeah, and if you could have done it without freeing a single slave, you would've."

"Not so," Lincoln countered. "You're angry."

"Yes, I have a lot to be angry about. You said: 'If I could save the Union by freeing all the slaves I would do it; and if I could save it by freeing some and leaving others alone I would also do that.' Your words, Mr. President."

"That was not my personal wish. If we didn't save the Union, slavery would have continued unabated."

"Slavery did continue 'unabated.'

"I tried to persuade the anti-black populace to support the Emancipation Proclamation."

"We're still trying. That's the crying shame of it all," lamented Charles.

"I told my cabinet a month before I wrote those words that I was going to issue the Emancipation Proclamation."

"What kind of policy is that?"

"My policy was to have no policy."

"You just tap-danced?"

"You might call it that."

"Politicians," Charles uttered, thinking again of Richie who went to war on the order of a president who tap danced around a poorly defined policy with no real plan for how to combat a fractured people determined to fight for the last inch of ground.

"Whatever the necessities of the hour demanded, that is what I've done," said Lincoln. "You have to be ready to adjust. To maintain a consistency for the sake of consistency is a fool's game. If there was policy to be made, I was the one who made it. My politics are like the old woman's dance — short and sweet."

Charles was wringing wet from sweat. The heat of the day had taken its toll. He saw a taxi coming his way and stuck out his arm, but the taxi sped past. The driver seemed to wave. He looked, Charles thought, a little like the Musician.

"You see that?" he asked Lincoln. "Taxi drove right by."

"Maybe he didn't see you," offered Lincoln.

"He saw me all right. He saw another black man who might rob him, saw a fare to a bad part of town." Charles wiped his forehead with his arm and walked off wondering how in the world this sort of thing could still happen. Lincoln was probably right, he thought, the guy didn't see *him*. It was that old soldier thing, seeing the *enemy* where they're not.

They couldn't get closer to the Capitol. It was fenced off, and there were several armed guards stationed.

"This doesn't look like we won the war. Are we under attack?"

"Every day it seems," said Charles.

"This looks like the women and children should be evacuated," said Lincoln surveying the concrete barriers and heavily-armed guards.

"This is what we get for being bull-headed, ignorant, and vague

175

about a supposed enemy — and underestimating that enemy."

"Your leaders should heed my mistakes," said Lincoln. "I was ill-prepared and a little too ready to rush to war — too optimistic."

"You were criticized too."

"Yes. Once the insurrection had begun, I was not fond of wily agitators."

"I suspect President Polk considered you to be a wily agitator for opposing the Mexican War. In fact, as President you arrested people for doing what you had done."

TWENTY - TWO

Later that night Charles drove out into the countryside. It was an adventure for Lincoln.

"I'd never get a general off of this contraption," Lincoln said, referring to the Bronco Charles drove. Before long Charles pulled into a parking lot at Gettysburg. The lot was just down the road from the well-maintained fields of Pickett's charge. Charles noticed that a few of the buildings, though, were in need of repair, and a soldier's statue was knocked off its pedestal.

The last time Lincoln was there, he had been invited to speak at the dedication of the National Soldiers' Cemetery. There had been makeshift graves that cool November day when he arrived. Now, he no longer recognized the place where 51,000 were killed or wounded. "Of the 14,000 Confederates who made that charge with Pickett, only half of them returned."

"The other half must be here," noted Charles looking out over the graveyard.

Lincoln mused, "It was July third. The Union Army withstood the charge. I was elated. It gave us a great opportunity to end the war right here. Pickett's charge took nearly an hour. Lee was hoping that victory would sway public opinion in the North against the war and me. He overplayed his poker hand. He didn't have the cards at Antietam either, but it was McClellan who folded. Then General Meade folded here, let Lee get away. Meade twiddled his thumbs the two weeks it took Lee to retreat. He did not appreciate the magnitude of the misfortune involved in letting Lee escape. Stood around like an old woman trying to shoo her geese across a creek. Maybe he didn't chase Lee because he was afraid he'd catch him. Maybe he didn't realize Lee was over-confidant, that he thought his army was invincible. None of us are."

Lincoln's mood was somber. The aftermath of Gettysburg with Lee's escape had left Lincoln in utter despair. He looked at Charles, and his mood seemed to change on a dime. "I composed a little ditty entitled, 'Gen. Lee's invasion of the North, written by himself':

> In eighteen sixty-three, with pomp
> And mighty swell,
> Me and Jeff's Confederacy, went
> Forth to sack Phil-del,
> The Yankees they got arter us, and
> Giv us particular hell,
> And we skedaddled back again,
> And didn't sack Phil-del.

Charles was surprised at the sudden change in Lincoln's demeanor. It was a sense of humor Charles both admired and envied.

178

As he stood looking over the famous battlefield, Charles remembered bringing Darlene and Richie out to see Gettysburg. It was a few weeks after Richie had challenged his dad to take a new look at Lincoln. Charles finally agreed to "revisit" his view of a man who had generally been exalted in the black community since the Civil War days.

"He wasn't superman, Dad," said Richie.

Charles wanted his son to see the site of the bloodiest battle of the Civil War, where so many lives were lost for a promise made by one man. Charles also wanted his boy to read the words of Lincoln's address to know it was one thing to learn them by rote and recite them unthinkingly, and an all together different experience to see the battlefield first-hand and to think about the words Lincoln wrote and why.

Charles wanted his son to see the place where Lincoln had made the speech that became the country's moral code. Charles had told his son the words had given him something to hold onto, to believe in, when all else was in despair, but the words had not lifted the people to a kinder, gentler country. This, he knew, was not Lincoln's fault. It seemed to Charles that America had stagnated, that it was slipping backward as a country. Charles felt the United States had not been dedicated enough to advancing the cause of all people.

When Charles was at his most positive, long before his son was killed, he wondered if Lincoln's words could regain a new energy? Could they inspire us to aspire to a better place? Could we meet the challenges that Lincoln set, the hopes and passion he had for all the people? Charles had engaged tourists on occasion to get a feel for how people felt, an informal survey, sort of a straw vote. He wished he could be more positive as he looked out across the battlefield that had inspired Lincoln's words.

"How many black soldiers were there?" Richie had asked his father.

"Blacks weren't part of the battle."

"Dad, I do appreciate Lincoln for what he did and for what he tried to do," Richie said, "but what you said about people at Princeton, Dad, is true about Lincoln — he put his pants on just like we do."

◆　◆　◆

"Lot of graves," Charles said, looking across the great expanse of the Gettysburg cemetery.

"Yes," nodded Lincoln. "Lot of blood spilled up to the ripe harvest, then allowed to go to waste."

Both men stood for awhile, thinking about the great cost of war.

"I always tried to be open and to the point with my generals. I wanted them to stay on the attack. Several of them had a case of the 'slows' however. I can't recall being madder than I was at Meade after the lost opportunity here at Gettysburg. He had Lee! Instead, the war went on another two years." Again Lincoln looked out across the field. "Our army held the war in the hollow of its hand and would not close it. I kept waiting and hoping. You pursue till you kill the enemy or he surrenders. Delay ruined us. Breath alone killed no rebels."

"You sound like a peace-loving man to me."

"To win a war, you have to fight. I wanted McClellan to attack Richmond, too, or give up the job. Admirable engineer, McClellan, but he had a special talent for a stationary engine. Had to have my photograph taken with him. We had to stand very still. I told them McClellan would have no trouble staying still, but I might be waving in the wind." Lincoln was shaking his head. "Kept saying he needed more men. If I had had a million men, I could not have got them to him in time. It reminds me of when the Capital itself was under attack, all I could do was anguish, looking out the window, wondering, 'Why don't they come? Why don't they come.' I never got an answer.

"Sending men to McClellan's army was like shoveling fleas across a barnyard, not half of them got there. Then his horses were fatigued. I didn't know what the horses of his army had done that fatigued anything. I begged him to attack Lee. I would have held his horse for him. But he wouldn't do it. You're right, I was too timid or I was simply too patient with him. Finally, I had no choice but to relieve him — something I should have done long before. If he wasn't going to use the army, I wanted to borrow it. I could've whipped Lee, myself."

"Yeah, you could have carried your ax into battle."

"What was I going to tell the people?" Lincoln put this out as a question to Charles.

"The buck stops here. You're the man."

"You're right. I knew if the war failed, I would be blamed."

"You're the one who hired all those bad generals. You could've fudged the numbers, told the people you were winning," Charles said sarcastically, remembering Vietnam and being distrustful of any positive news out of Iraq.

Lincoln looked questionably at him. "I could not fathom such a thing. I had to keep some standard of principle fixed within myself, but I was determined not to surrender the game without playing every card available."

"You weren't playing with a full deck."

"At times people tell me things I do not wish to hear," said Lincoln.

"But you have such a great capacity for unpleasant things it doesn't matter," said Charles, smiling.

"I am trying to preserve my temper, by avoiding irritants, so far as practicable."

"You can't avoid me, Lincoln. You can't fire me like you did your generals."

"What I cannot do, I will not do. I struggled for ten days once to get General Burnside, who replaced McClellan, to move to support General Rosecrans, who was somewhat confused and stunned like a duck hit on the head. Burnside declared he'd do it, yet he steadily moved the other way. Made me doubt whether I was awake or dreaming. Some days I wondered if our trouble was in our case, not our generals."

"You mean 'our case' being slavery? You were backtracking again? Defending the slave owners again?"

"The Constitution made it necessary," said Lincoln a little testily.

They walked out on a hill overlooking the moonlit graves.

"It's quieter than I remember." Lincoln was overcome with emotion yet again and took a few steps away to gather his thoughts. He found himself walking toward the little knoll where he had delivered his Gettysburg Address. "I finished talking before some knew I had started."

They walked down the slight slope of the hill among the grave markers.

"A lot of men who prayed to God are laid out in this field," said Charles.

"Any religion that sets men to rebel and fight against their government, because, as they think, that government doesn't help some men eat their bread on the sweat of other men's faces, is not the sort of religion upon which people can get to heaven. I don't care how much they pray."

"Every army that ever fought in the history of the world has claimed to have God on its side," said Charles shaking his head.

"Both sides prayed to the same God," replied Lincoln. "One side had to be wrong. Maybe God had something else in mind. I wanted God on my side, but I needed Kentucky more. Besides, I can love God with all my heart and soul, but if I don't love you what good does it do me?" Lincoln had turned to look at Charles.

The cemetery seemed a good place to rest one's head away from the heat and humidity of the Capital, so Charles and Lincoln laid their weary bodies on a slight incline and rested their heads on clumps of grass. There was a flash of heat lightning.

Loving his son so much and no longer having him was the hardest thing Charles had ever faced, including the Viet Cong. He looked at the stars recalling a passage from Shakespeare:

> Take him and cut him out in little stars
> And he will make the face of heav'n so fine
> That all the world will be in love with night
> And pay no worship to the garish sun.

Neither man could sleep. A cloud passed across the full moon.

"After I came home from Vietnam, I pitched a tent in the back yard. I couldn't sleep inside."

"The sleepless nights of sorrow," Lincoln said glancing at Charles. "Nothing more like eternity than a sleepless night. Unless it's two people and a ham." He could tell that his joke was not appreciated. "It's a big ham." Lincoln held his arms apart to indicate the size.

"You're the ham," Charles joked.

"My wife would agree with you. She says my jokes are like a long train ride, and you think the trip will never end."

They were still for a bit until Lincoln once again broke the silence. "I fell asleep at my desk and had a premonition. I was in a little boat with all the people of this nation gathered around in their own little boats. We were headed toward a dark and infinite shore."

"It's called Iraq," muttered Charles.

The persistent hooting of an owl aroused Lincoln to recall from memory a poem of long ago:

> Here, where the lonely hooting owl
> Sends forth his midnight moans,
> Fierce wolves shall o'er my carcass growl,
> Or buzzards pick my bones.

> No fellow-man shall learn my fate,
> Or where my ashes lie;
> Unless by beasts drawn round their bait,
> Or by the ravens cry.

> Yes! I've resolved the deed to do,
> And this the place to do it:
> This heart I'll rush a dagger through
> Though I in hell should rue it!

"You can keep those depressing poems to yourself, Lincoln. I don't need to hear them. I feel lousy enough as it is. I don't know what the solution is, but you're not helping."

"You'll either die or get better," said Lincoln to the dark sky.

"So you say. Thanks."

Eventually, Lincoln mentioned a dream he'd had the night before. He let it hang in the air until Charles finally asked, "You just going to torture me?"

Lincoln smiled and said, "It was the same dream I had before the victories at Antietam, Murfreesboro, Vicksburg, and Gettysburg."

Charles refuted Lincoln's assessment. "Murfreesboro was no victory, Antietam was a half-assed job, and so was Gettysburg. You said so yourself."

◆   ◆   ◆

"I know, I know," lamented Lincoln. "But when Vicksburg surrendered to General Grant, I was overjoyed. It was great, great! I had been in deep despair before I learned of Grant's taking Vicksburg. The news was a tremendous relief."

"You thought Grant had made a mistake."

"Yes, when Grant reached the outskirts of Vicksburg, then went below and took Port-Gibson, I thought he should go down river and join General Banks; and when he turned northward, east of the Big Black River, I feared it was a mistake. It turned out General Grant was right and I was wrong."

"But that didn't stop you from offering advice."

"Whatever advice I gave was as suggestion only."

They lay on the grass exhausted, comforted by the bright, peaceful stars above and the quiet all around.

"We aren't clear of the woods, but the signs look better," said Lincoln.

"We must be reading different stars."

They both understood that hindsight has a harsh glow.

"I told you if the war failed I'd be blamed."

"You and your high-toned holier-than-thou ideals."

"High toned, holier than thou?"

"That nobody gives a crap about, except maybe to forget the Gettysburg Address a lot faster than they took to memorize it."

"I ought to be blamed . . . ."

"You got that right."

". . . if I could've done better. You think I could've done better. I think I could not do better; therefore I blame you for blaming me."

"I knew you would get around to that. It's all my fault. Politicians!"

"You are not the only one dissatisfied," said Lincoln. "Many of my party wanted to get rid of me. I was half disposed to gratify them."

They laid in silence looking at the stars, contemplating the heavens and the great mystery beyond.

"Feel that? The quiet."

"Yes," Lincoln said.

"Make you feel lost?"

"No, it makes me feel alive," replied Lincoln.

"Too quiet," said Charles, reacting as a soldier in Vietnam. It had been years since he had slept outside. "You forget this is just someplace to hide, to attack, because the enemy is out there, just can't see them. Lookouts no good, no beacons of smoke, no fires by night, no fire hoses. Have to sleep with one eye open. Just like Brer Rabbit."

"Better to sleep with both eyes closed because you could get twice as much sleep that way," joked Lincoln.

"Also get dead that way," Charles replied.

Charles and Lincoln watched heat lightening light up the night sky.

"Where's the thunder?" asked Charles.

Lincoln pointed to his head. "I have been wondering about Lee's frame of mind when he led his troops into a battle that saw men rushing to their sure suicide. Was it the act of a desperate man? Was Lee blinded by his own depression? Did that lull him into making such drastic decisions on the battlefield? Despite impressive but very costly prior victories, I wonder if Lee was really so sure of victory at Gettysburg? Because of depleted man-power, maybe he saw Gettysburg as a last gasp for the South rather than certain defeat for the Union. Or did Lee feel that a bold attack on northern soil would be too much for the northern citizens who had not been exposed to the grim face of war. Guess I'll never know."

"I certainly have no answers about the decisions you leaders make. Hell, 7,000 men were killed or wounded down at Cold Harbor. What was that about?"

"To win a war you have to fight," said Lincoln.

"The war was already won."

"It was an ill-advised battle," lamented Lincoln.

"Stupid's what it was," said Charles.

Stupid was how Charles felt about the political arguments over the war in Iraq. Nothing was going to bring back his son. He hated hearing "numbers," how many were lost in this battle or that battle. When remembered in "body counts," soldiers were deprived of their identity. "These are lives, not numbers," Charles had told Darlene. And what about the 100,000 dead civilians of Iraq and Afghanistan?" he'd asked.

Charles looked up at the stars wondering what was on the other side. "The planet Mercury turns in a way that brings heat and cold, light and dark at the same time. I always thought that was a perfect description of a battlefield."

"A very good observation."

"What do you call a black man with a Ph.D?"

Lincoln wasn't sure what Charles was asking.

"A nigger," Charles said flatly. "Never told a 'darky' joke?"

Lincoln was quiet.

"Cat got your tongue?"

"I was known to tell a joke or two," said Lincoln his voice rising slightly. Charles asked Lincoln if he had ever used the "n" word.

"Maybe once or twice. I don't know."

"Know what a nigger is?"

Lincoln was quiet.

"Scum. Trash. The dirt off your shoe."

Like the earlier taxi incident that left him stranded on the curb in front of the Capitol, Charles knew this negative thinking was something that should not cross his mind today. But there were those damned redneck prosecutors with the nooses on their ties! Charles could not let this go.

He tried to tell himself that the noose left in the lap of Lincoln's statue that morning was nothing to get carried away about. For an instant he had been caught off guard, was angry. He hadn't wanted to even touch the noose, but he couldn't just leave it there. It was no big deal, no conspiracy, he told himself. This was not done by some angry white guy who got passed over for a promotion because of affirmative action. It was probably just some kid thinking it was a cool thing to do on America's birthday. Whoever did it knew what the response would be.

"Don't get the wrong idea. We'll look into it. Issue a memo or two." Charles had heard those arguments over the years. It's not like the noose had somebody's name on it. No, Charles said to himself, it was just meant for all black people.

Maybe, Charles thought, he should give the noose to the police or F.B.I. He could hear Willie from Philly, saying he needed to go out and kick some cracker ass.

"Don't keep sticking your head in the sand. You're getting shined on, Shakespeare. Don't be quoting any more crap from your famous and greatest. I ain't buying."

TWENTY - THREE

Charles must have fallen asleep for a brief time. The sound of explosives aroused him, and he woke smelling blood in the water. Suddenly more explosions rocked the night air and Charles was spun into a frenzy all around him. The fireworks were mixed in with a Civil War re-enactment. Soldiers were running around in a chaos of activity while a choir sang and a full orchestra played. There were drums pounding and bugles blaring. The Marine Band was playing *The Battle Hymn of the Republic*. For Charles, the swirling commotion was too close to home. In a daze he jumped up. Lincoln rose, too, standing beside Charles, who was frozen in the turmoil of the re-enactment and his vivid memory. Mayhem prevailed all around them.

In Charles' eyes and mind, Union and Confederate troops were now mixed with Vietnam soldiers and the Viet Cong. It was a surreal battle scene, close up fighting, hand to hand combat. A literal blood frenzy. Some Confederates were wearing bits and pieces of

Union uniforms. A few Viet Cong were wearing Marine green. Explosions ripped through the night. Tracer fire erupted along the ground nearby. Charles and Lincoln stood stock still and watched, observers to the awful brutality of war.

Private Charles Huggins outpost was under intense fire. He and Willie from Philly knelt behind sandbags on the fireline. "All hell's breakin' loose, Shakespeare."

"Gettin' it from all sides, it seems," Huggins said nervously as voices resounded down the line.

"Destroy the signal codes! Burn everything!"

"Incoming! Holy Shit!"

Willie from Philly sent forth a burst of fire from his M-16 into the treeline, chopping a couple of them in half.

"Happy New Year!" Willie shouted as he dropped, again, down behind the sandbags. "They could've just sent a card. They didn't need to come all this way," he joked about the Viet Cong. He lit a cigarette. A bullet whizzed right past his head. Huggins reached over, grabbed the cigarette from Willie's mouth, and put it out.

"You trying to get us killed?"

Willie fired his pistol blindly several times. Huggins quoted Shakespeare.

> In peace there's nothing so become's a man
> As modest stillness and humility.
> But when the blast of war blows in our ears,
> Then imitate the action of the tiger.

Charles looked at Lincoln. "I told you we could lock and load and quote Shakespeare."

◆ ◆ ◆

Willie yelled, "Oh for God's sake, Shakespeare, let's go kill something!"

Just then an order was screamed far down the line — "Bayonets!"

Young Huggins echoed the order at the top of his lungs. "Fix bayonets!"

"Guess we get to see what a commie looks like close up," Willie said, while both secured their bayonets in place. "Remember — spring, don't hop, Shakespeare." They had been taught that was the essence of bayonet fighting, going into a crouch and then thrusting the blade into the enemy. "I don't want to see any tears on that blade. And one more thing, Shakespeare. Keep to the rhythm and you won't get lost." Willie laughed and then looked to the sky. "How about it God? No pain and no screaming. Just lights out." The enemies were surging toward them. "If it moves what do we do?"

"We kill it."

"What was that, Shakespeare? I couldn't hear you."

"We kill it!" Huggins shouted, then softly to himself, "Didn't mean to die today, Mom. Sorry. Forgive me. I love you." He then reached into his pocket and pulled out the chain with the Virgin Mary statue the home bound soldier had given him as he was getting off the plane. He slid it around his neck.

◆ ◆ ◆

Charles and Lincoln joined in the fray of the re-enactment battle, Charles, once again a soldier, a marine, and Lincoln, the war president. The Marine Band rallied the troops with *Up Soldiers and Fight*.

"Lock and load," Charles shouted.

"If I had just fifty thousand troops here now, I could close the war in two weeks," said a frustrated Lincoln. Charles had heard forecasts like that in Vietnam. Willie and young Huggins screamed war cries, leaping up with guns blazing. Bodies fell all around.

"Let's kick ass!" commanded Willie.

"Kill the bastards, kill them," young Huggins responded in kind.

"Don't be 'showing your color,' as my Mama said," Willie advised.

Charles was taken back by the ferocity of the passion of his younger self. Just then Lincoln stood to his full height.

"Get down," commanded Charles to Lincoln.

"I can take care of myself."

Charles pulled at Lincoln's coat, but Lincoln brushed away Charles' arm.

"For an awkward fellow, I'm pretty sure-footed."

"But your ice ain't colder, remember," said Charles again grabbing hold of Lincoln.

Lincoln pushed Charles down and strode out into the midst of the fighting. He seemed to be taking energy from the Marine band's music.

"In your hands, my dissatisfied fellow-countrymen, and not in mine, is the momentous issue of civil war."

"They don't want to hear any speech!" Charles shouted at Lincoln.

"It is my duty to suppress an insurrection. The . . ."

Charles got in Lincoln's face.

"What is this 'insurrection crap.' This is war!"

"We are not enemies but friends," a flustered Lincoln managed.

"This is no cocktail party!" Charles yelled.

"In giving freedom to the slave, we assure freedom to the free — honorable alike in what we give and what we preserve," said an undeterred Lincoln.

There was a lull in the action. Charles tackled Lincoln and wrestled him to the ground. They rolled back and forth in locked combat.

"We cannot escape history," said Lincoln, almost lamenting.

"We haven't!" Charles assured him.

"I cannot betray the peoples' trust, nor count the chances of my own life." With that, Lincoln managed to get up and again start toward the action.

Charles ran and tackled Lincoln anew pinning him to the ground. Lincoln struggled to get up. "I have no moral right to shrink."

"Don't get uppity with me, Lincoln."

"Though passion may have strained, it must not break our bonds of affection," Lincoln called to the troops of all sides.

"Bonds of affection? Look around you, Lincoln!" Lincoln continued . . . .

"The mystic chords of memory, stretching from every battle-field . . ."

At that moment Huggins nearly drowned out Lincoln's words. "THRUST! JAB! KILL!"

". . . and patriot grave . . ."

Lincoln and Charles were now surrounded by soldiers from both wars.

". . . to every living heart and hearthstone," Lincoln went on.

"You're flailing, Lincoln," said Charles, letting him go.

". . . all over this broad land, will yet swell the chorus of the Union, when again touched, as surely they will be, by the better angels of our nature." By now Lincoln was pleading to be heard.

"Yeah, those better angels are right behind us," said Charles looking at the mayhem around them.

At that point it seemed as though all fighting stopped — with the combatants laughing uproariously.

"You hear that laughing?" Lincoln was astounded.

"They're laughing at you" said Charles. " 'The better angels of our nature.' This isn't a walk in the park." A sudden explosion hit close to them. The soldiers resumed their torrid fighting. "This is bloody war!" Another explosion hit.

"Ballots are the rightful and peaceful successors of bullets," said a weary Lincoln as he viewed the scene.

"Ballots?" Charles wished he could laugh.

"Seek ye first the political kingdom and all others shall be added to it."

"There are no ballots. No thought. Just death."

The advancing troops surged around Lincoln and Charles. Cannon fire erupted from the ridge. The Confederates were being ripped by explosions.

"Where are they? Where's it coming from?" said a confused Huggins.

"If it ain't in Marine Corps green, blast it till it can't be seen," Willie screamed. Several black soldiers in marine combat fatigues rushed by Lincoln. He watched them, then looked at Charles.

"You saw right. Black soldiers."

A Vietnam Marine suddenly fell dead in front of Lincoln. Huggins fell to his knees and bent over his fallen comrade, shocked to see a bullet hole the size of a dime in the Marine's forehead.

◆ ◆ ◆

Charles, watching, said, "Ever killed a man, Lincoln?"

"No. . . . not by my own hand." In an effort to distract, Lincoln went on to tell a story of how shortly before he was eight years old, a flock of wild turkeys had approached their cabin. He shot through a crack and killed one of them. "I never pulled a trigger on any larger game."

Charles watched young Huggins looking at a photo from the dead enemy's helmet, a photo of a family.

"You learn to hate killing from a turkey, then go and become its worst enemy?"

Lincoln seemed puzzled.

"Thanksgiving Day," explained Charles.

"That was one of mine," Lincoln nodded.

"Yeah. Now we celebrate it around a turkey."

"Odd, how things turn out."

"Especially if you're a turkey," said Charles. What he didn't say was that he felt his son had been a turkey who had been plucked, cleaned, and dressed. Richie had been poorly trained, sent to a war he had no business fighting.

Charles looked down into a ditch where the dead of all sides lay piled atop one another. He could hear moans coming from the wounded. "Is this what you call duty? How do you deal with death, Lincoln?"

"We all have to die sometime. Not much difference between today and tomorrow."

"Most of us prefer tomorrow, especially if you are only twenty-one years old!"

"Old men make war, the young fight them. Emotion can kill you. Sometimes you feel so strongly about an issue that is in opposition to what someone else feels just as strongly and when there is no give on either side . . ."

"War happens," finished Charles, remembering the same thought Alice had earlier expressed to him.

TWENTY - FOUR

"Nothing's more precious than freedom and independence."
"I said that," said Lincoln.
"So did Ho Chi Minh."

◆　◆　◆

The advancing Confederate troops surged around Lincoln and Charles toward the waiting Union troops on the high ridge across the field. Canon fire erupted from the ridge. Explosions again ripped into the Confederate lines.

"It's a damn massacre," said Willie. Overwhelmed, he had stopped firing his gun and was taking in the slaughter all around him. Young Huggins pulled him down while continuing to fire his M-16.

◆　◆　◆

Lincoln was frustrated as he addressed a telegram from one of his generals. Waving the telegram in the air, Lincoln angrily said to Charles, "If he is being besieged, how does he dispatch me? Why did he not leave before being besieged? How does he know the rebel forces are large?" Lincoln angrily tore up the telegram. "Generals have a tendency to inflate the enemy's number."

"We could use a little help, God," said young Huggins.

"God don't work here," replied Willie as a barrage of bullets enveloped them.

"Faith makes right," said young Huggins.

Despite the turmoil, Willie could not help laughing. "White makes right, Shakespeare."

Young soldier Huggins had found it harder to ignore these comments from Willie. He had seen white soldiers seemingly being favored when it came to "R&R." Some whites seemed to get discharges sooner. Perhaps, he thought, especially when in the heat of battle, his brother Terry had been right. He should have stayed home to fight the battle there, but Uncle Sam would not have allowed that.

"We're outflanked and out numbered. Let's get out of here," yelled Willie. They began to retreat.

Lincoln and Charles stood in the midst of retreating soldiers. Lincoln asked, "What's happening?"

"What's it look like?"

The disheartened, torn, and tattered soldiers continued their retreat.

◆　◆　◆

A Union major rode down on horseback, calling out to the General, "The line will not hold, and once broken . . ."

199

Lincoln looked at the general sitting astride his horse. "Continue to fight, General," ordered Lincoln. "If you don't stand up and fight for what is yours, the Fourth of July won't amount to a hill of beans!"

Charles laughed, "Oh, it won't quite dwindle away. You can still celebrate. You can even go so far as to read the Declaration of Independence as an interesting memorial of the dead past."

"I believe that's my line, soldier," Lincoln, picking up a spent shell from off the ground. "Old wadding left to rot on the battlefield after the victory is won. July Fourth will still be a great day for burning firecrackers!" He threw the spent shell nearly hitting the general.

The general flinched and his horse reared, "I deserve removal, Sir, for not standing up when my men were in no condition to fight."

"You seem to imply, General, that I forced you into battle," countered Lincoln.

"No, Sir."

"It is no pleasure to me to triumph over anyone," said Lincoln. And then, so there could be no misunderstanding as to how he felt, Lincoln added, "But if slavery continues so must the war. We must be like the shepherd's charges and stay the course by staying together. Let us remember the fallen and for their sake be sure the fight will continue. Good soldiers march on!"

. With that, the general reared his horse yelling,"Fire!"

"If you can hold your position, we shall have the enemy yet," said a reinvigorated Lincoln.

The general slashed his sword toward the onrushing Confederate Army. The Union lines opened fire. A hail of lead laced into the Confederate troops.

"It's near impossible to get a general off his horse," complained

Lincoln to Charles. "Their rear is glued to the saddle. To win a war you have to fight." Lincoln punctuated his words by an emphatic downward motion of his clenched right fist.

"You keep saying that."

"Grant understood that."

"Maybe that's why you didn't fire him."

"He who has the right needs not to fear," said Lincoln.

"And losing 15,000 men in an hour's time was right?"

"Grant's a fighting man. I'm lucky to have had him," said Lincoln.

"He was a drinker," Charles noted.

"Exaggerated. But if I'd known his brand. I would have sent it to all my other generals," Lincoln said, only half joking.

"Grant liked Kentucky bourbon, Old Crow," said Charles.

"Where were you when I needed you?"

"Down on the plantation because you were too willy-nilly." He then reminded Lincoln that when Sherman took Atlanta, "He handed you the re-election on a platter of ashes."

"Again, exaggerated," said Lincoln.

"Depends which side of the line you're on," replied Charles.

Lincoln turned, "It was a war!"

"The Great Emancipator won the war."

"It gives me no pleasure to triumph over anyone," Lincoln said.

"Didn't you go into Richmond after victory and sit in Jeff Davis' chair?"

Lincoln let out a long sigh. "I refuse to indulge in triumphalism, righteousness, or vilification of the foe."

"Are you saying you didn't enjoy victory?"

"I think I was just so relieved and elated that Richmond was in Union hands that I sat in the first chair I came to."

"You were celebrating."

"I was of two minds. The cause was certainly just, but the cheering was fleeting, the victory was not triumphant."

Huggins and Willie were in the midst of chaos, artillery exploding all around them. Their unit was being overrun by the Viet Cong. Huggins yelled commands as he retreated. It was hand to hand fighting amid confused running and screaming. Huts were ablaze.

"Our cause is destined to triumph," said Lincoln.

"Our cause? Your cause. I told you I don't want to hear about causes."

Suddenly out of nowhere a squad of dazzling high school cheerleaders appeared dressed as Lincoln, complete with megaphones and pom poms. They crashed the re-enactment party with anti-war signs and a vibrant cheer. The fighting came to a complete halt.

"Give us a P!"

"P"

"Give us a E!"

"E"

"Give us an A!"

"A"

"Give us a C!"

"C"

"Give us a E!"

"E"

"What does that spell?"

Some in the crowd of spectators yelled, "Peace." Others started booing. At that point, the cheerleaders were tackled and carried off the field by the various troops. The battlefield was reset, soldiers took their place, fighting was ready to resume full out. Lincoln yelled encouragement to the troops as he walked among them.

"Every edge must be made to cut."

"They can't hear you, Lincoln," said Charles.

"Stand firm, as with a chain of steel," said Lincoln, continuing to rally the surrounding troops.

"There are no cheap victories," said Charles with no energy for an old tired line.

"Hold on with a bull dog grip."

"Yeah, do it for your people," said Charles sarcastically.

"Chew and choke as much as possible. Victory here could end the war. If a man can't skin he must hold a leg while somebody else does." Charles gave a double take to Lincoln's expression and went him one better.

"Saddle up, ladies. Don't stop to pick your nose, fire to the left and run to the right."

"It is a question of legs. Put in all the speed you can. Do not let the enemy off without being hurt!"

The troops slowly started off.

"Beware of rashness, beware of rashness," cautioned Lincoln. "I would not take the risk of being entangled upon the river, like an ox jumped half over a fence, and liable to be torn by dogs, front and rear, without a fair chance to gore one way or the other."

Charles didn't know whether to laugh or cry on hearing Lincoln's line. The Union drummer boy and a fife player marched by playing the cavalry anthem *Gary Owen*.

"You heard the man," yelled Huggins, "move it out. Let's raise some hell! Duty calls! Victory or death!"

"Make that victory or get hurt pretty bad!" yelled Willie from Philly. "Action!" Appreciating Willie's sense of humor in this dire situation, they all picked up the pace.

◆ ◆ ◆

The music cut through, blending with the sound of gun and canon fire. Lincoln, stirred by the music, started to sing:

> Come on boys, and grab your sabers
> Come on boys, and ride with me.

Charles joined in the singing with a false exuberance:

> Give the cry of Gary Owen, Make
> your place in history.

Young soldier Huggins and Willie from Philly joined in:

> Come on, boys, and grab your sabers.
> Come on boys and ride with me.

Charles then saw Richie join the singing:

> Give the cry of Gary Owen,
> Make your place in history.

Explosions, fireworks, and screams erupted as chaos consumed them all. Young Huggins raced through the underbrush. Tracerfire ripped through the trees. Rockets exploded nearby. Screams and yelled commands echoed off the hills. Young Huggins was hit in his right leg, arm, and side. He turned to see a Viet Cong soldier step out behind a tree. For a second they were both surprised. Their eyes locked. They slashed at each other with their bayonets. The Viet Cong's rifle butt hit the private in the face. He spun and fell, sink-ing to his knees, stunned and bleeding. He struggled to retrieve his pistol from his boot, one he had kept in case he found himself with no recourse. The Viet Cong rammed his bayonet into Huggins' gut but it only went part way. The blade caught on his belt buckle. Both men were not sure what had happened, but Huggins managed to retrieve his pistol and aimed at the Viet Cong's head. There was the moment when they both knew what was about to happen. Huggins fired and the enemy slammed backward to the ground. Private Huggins slumped over, unconscious.

◆　◆　◆

"Funny, I wasn't scared, didn't even mind being shot at," said Charles, "but it really sucked getting shot. I was afraid I wouldn't be able to dance again." The image of him dancing with young Darlene at his mother's going-away party flashed before him. "Remember the good times because that's all you got to carry you through."

Lincoln understood.

◆　◆　◆

At that moment a huge blast rocked the ground. Young Huggins awoke to find he was still alive. He called out for Willie, but there was no answer. He struggled to his feet and commenced to look for his friend among the carnage. He went from body to body, a mixture of rebels, yankees, Viet Cong, Marines from both Vietnam and Iraq.

"Willie, Willie. Where are you?" He hobbled into a tiny clearing and saw Willie kneeling at the feet of the enemy. Willie had been shot in the shoulder, and the Viet Cong soldier stabbed him in the stomach with a bayonet. Willie clutched the end of the blade. The Viet Cong soldier kicked Willie's shoulder back knocking his body off the blade. Willie fell backward with a strangled cry. The Viet Cong raised his rifle to finish Willie off. Huggins screamed and half ran, his wounded leg dragging along the ground into the clearing. The Viet Cong spun to fire at him, but too late. He was ripped by young Huggins' bullets and fell back into the brush. Huggins hurried to Willie.

"You got to work on that war cry," gargled Willie breathing raggedly, blood spitting from his lips.

"I'll do that," said young Huggins, struggling to lift Willie.

"Oh God, no, don't. I'm done."

Young Huggins got Willie seated on a wooden crate. He took the chain with the little statue of the Virgin Mary from around his neck and slid it over Willie's head.

"Shut your mouth. You got to have faith in something. This little lady says you can't die tonight. Not your time. You got things to do, places to go, people to see."

Willie tried to laugh. "You're a strange man, Charlie Huggins."

"Keep to the rhythm and you won't get lost."

Huggins sat down beside Willie and tied a tourniquet around his own wounded leg. They were surrounded by fog, smoldering wreckage, ashes — and bodies. Pigs were eating at the corpses.

"Never expected you'd be my savior."

"We're going home, Willie. We fought our fight, and now we're done."

"How many times I gotta tell you? We ain't got no home. No country. No room at the inn. Our house is a house of cards. We got some bad carpenters."

"We're going to build our own house. You and me. Just hold on."

"Don't shed no tear for me. I'm outta here."

◆　◆　◆

Lincoln stood among the carnage of the broken aftermath of the battle. Bodies lay everywhere. Lincoln watched the medical teams load the living onto stretchers.

"Give me the latest news. . . . Please give me the latest news."

Lincoln's requests were met with vacant stares.

"I greatly fear another failure . . . . My God, my God, what will the people say?"

"When is war ever over?" asked Charles.

"When the defeated party says it's over," Lincoln answered.

The sounds of battle subside leaving only the soft and close singing of soldiers.

> And we'll rally round the flag, boys
> We'll rally once again
> Shouting the battle cry of freedom.
> And our battle cry shall be
> Not one man shall be a slave
> Shouting the battle cry of freedom.

Charles turned to see a body lying in the mass of rubble from the explosion. His eyes filled with tears, but he stepped closer and the dead soldier's face became to Charles the face of his own dead son.

> And we'll rally round the flag, boys
> We'll rally once again
> Shouting the battle cry of freedom.

And our battle cry shall be
Not one man shall be a slave
Shouting the battle cry of freedom.

Charles knelt to put his arms around the soldier's broken body.

The Musician, dressed in a grab bag of military uniforms from all the different soldiers, played *Ellsworth's Funeral March* on his fife. Lincoln bent down to another fallen soldier — Private Huggins.

"You hurt bad, soldier?"

"Didn't die."

"No lost limbs."

"Just my mind, I've lost."

Lincoln touched the young private's head and then slowly raised his tall frame and looked at the carnage. "The nation's condition is not what any man devised or expected. God alone can claim it."

"Hear that, God? Man says it's all your fault," Charles shouted, still holding his son.

Lincoln spoke again: "By His mere quiet power, he could have either saved or destroyed the Union without a human contest. Yet the contest began. And having begun, He could give the final victory to either side any day. Yet the contest proceeds."

"When he gets up there, God, paint him black and send him back," yelled Charles.

Lincoln looked down at Charles, "Surely God intends some great good to follow this mighty convulsion. When peace comes . . . "

"If," Charles moaned.

"It will come . . . and when it does, when the storm shall be past . . ." Lincoln looked out across the battlefield. The sound of the battle was distant and muted. Medics loaded Willie onto a stretcher.

The little statue of the Virgin Mary was still around his neck. Young Huggins stood nearby, his arm in a sling, his chest and leg bandaged. He used a crutch to balance himself on his good leg.

"So you're headed home?" Willie asked.

"Damn right," said young Huggins.

"You give my best to that sweet little Darlene."

"I'll do that. You take care of yourself."

"I'll give it a try."

They clasped hands and soldier Huggins helped Willie put on a pair of sunglasses.

"I'll see you stateside," said Huggins.

"Count on it. I'll be watching."

Willie pulled out his harmonica and tried to play.

"Lincoln, Willie kept me alive. I found out he re-upped for another tour. He died pulling a little Vietnamese girl out of a hut that got set on fire by shelling. They gave him a medal."

"The valiant never taste of death but once," said Lincoln.

"*Julius Caesar*. Dangerous play for a king or a president," replied Charles.

TWENTY - FIVE

Charles found himself once again staring at his image in the reflecting pool in front of Lincoln's Memorial. He had always found a sense of serenity around the pool. That was no longer the case. He couldn't imagine why he had been so certain about going to Vietnam. He had been ready to kill for his absolute sureness about what he thought was right. But at such a young age, he wondered, how could he possibly have known what was right or wrong? He simply didn't hear the other side. He couldn't help himself. Neither, it seemed, could his son. Charles heard Lincoln's voice behind him.

"There are some black men, like you, who will remember that with clenched teeth, a steady eye, and well-poised bayonet, you helped your country to a great consummation."

"There was and is no consummation," Charles said bitterly.

Lincoln took a moment and then quoted his favorite writer.

"Tis a consummation devoutly to be wish'd."

"*Hamlet.*"

That was an easy one for Charles. The contest was on as they traded lines in rapid fire.

"To be, or not to be . . ." Lincoln replied not missing a beat, ". . .

". . . that is the question" countered Charles. He then continued on, posing a most personal question.

> Whether tis nobler in the mind to suffer
> The slings and arrows of outrageous fortune,
> Or to take arms against a sea of troubles
> And by opposing end them.
> To die, to sleep
> No more, and by a sleep to say we end
> The heart-ache and the thousand natural shocks
> That flesh is heir to . . .

Charles shrugged when he finished quoting one of his favorite passages. He looked at Lincoln with a desperate, painful and vulnerable face.

". . . 'tis a consummation devoutly to be wish'd," said Charles.

"Shakespeare was one of those geniuses who could dip into the infinite as far and as deep as he liked," Lincoln observed.

◆　◆　◆

Charles recalled the day he limped off the plane in San Francisco. He hadn't expected a parade, didn't need one. Families and friends had cheered and embraced them. Darlene and Charles' mother were there. He kissed Darlene and held her for a long time. He had to break away because she was squeezing him so hard it hurt his tender wounds. They both laughed. Off to the side, there had been protesters shouting insults at the returning vets who had done their duty, served their time. Charles had been decorated.

"I was confused by the reception. I thought I had earned the right not to fear, not to be hated, not to be called a baby killer."

"To be wounded in the house of one's friends is perhaps the most grievous affliction that can befall a man," said Lincoln.

"No," Charles said, "it's to lose a son to another useless war."

"Grief can drive you mad," Lincoln reflected to himself.

Charles remembered he had been glad Willie wasn't there that day, getting off the plane, having to endure the taunts. Willie would have heckled the protesters right back, giving them some of their own medicine, though they were only protesting a war Charles too had found useless. Willie, in one of those hunkered down quiet moments when the war had taken pause, had ventured to Huggins that perhaps when they got home, the country would be different, they would really be truly free. But for the longest time after Vietnam, Charles did not feel free. For years there was little sense of elation at being home. He had never felt more at sea in his own country.

◆　◆　◆

The Vietnam Veterans Memorial Wall stretched out like a glimmering black sash across the green of the Mall, across the conscience of America. Charles knew many people visited the Wall after dark. Some, like himself, did not at first want to come at all, afraid the Wall would be what some people described, "a black gash of shame."

"Darlene made me visit the first time," he told Lincoln. "It was the dedication. I laid my medal with Willie. It was still hard for me to realize he was gone. He was the sort of fast-talking guy you thought would never die. More men were killed in my regiment than killed in any regiment, North or South, at Gettysburg. But who gives a plugged nickel about a place you can't pronounce?"

"I should have a wall for my soldiers."

"You'd need ten walls," said Charles.

Lincoln was quiet for a long time. He seemed to be trying to make sense of it all. Then the enormity of it came crushing down.

"Like my war, your war was a waste, a terrible, terrible waste," said Charles.

"It was, if there was no difference between hogs and Negroes."

"There was. Hogs cost more."

Lincoln nodded his head, taking in the awful truth of that statement. He looked for a long time at the black wall, walking up and down the length of it. "It's as if they each have reached into the core of my soul." On the ground in front of a section of the Wall, he spotted a golf club, a teddy bear, a woman's red shoe, and a small wooden cross. He read aloud the note that was attached to the cross.

> . . . we will eat our meal in fear,
> and sleep In the affliction of these
> terrible dreams, That shake us
> nightly; better be with the dead,
> Than on the torture of the mind to
> lie in restless ecstasy.

Charles waited a moment and then said, "*Macbeth*."

"After the dedication of the Vietnam Wall was over," he related, "I was glad Darlene had made me come. She insisted afterwards that we pay you a visit. I hadn't been to your Memorial since my mother, brother and I went to hear Reverend King speak. I bragged to Darlene that I knew the Gettysburg Address by heart. She said, 'All right, Hot Shot, do it.' I did pretty well. Then she gave me a second try and that time I nailed it. What's more, I listened to the words. You have to say those words out loud. Anyway, your speech gave me hope, like Reverend King's did. It's hard when you lose hope. There's not a worse feeling except — losing your child."

TWENTY - SIX

It was well after midnight by the time Charles got back home. He was leaning against a wall staring at his son's closed bedroom door. Lincoln was leaning back in a kitchen chair, his legs stretched out before him, talking about how he hoped he had made some marks for the cause of civil liberty. Charles' laugh might have perturbed Lincoln, but he didn't show it.

"You think you can make me a present of liberty?"

"The Constitution does that," said Lincoln. "No person shall be deprived of liberty without due process of law."

Charles asked Lincoln about his words of not being in favor of the political and social equality for the black race.

"My politics rest upon the principle of civil and political equality of both races."

"Horse manure. That's what that principle is."

"That principle is the foundation of who we are as a people, and you have a right to claim that principle as though you're blood of the blood, and flesh of the flesh of the men who wrote the Declaration."

"I probably am flesh of the flesh and blood of the blood of some of those men."

Lincoln smiled at Charles' joke. "That principle is the immortal emblem of humanity."

"White man's humanity," countered Charles, his emotions wired.

"It's a pledge to all people of all colors everywhere," insisted Lincoln.

"You are on record, Lincoln! 'I am not, nor ever have been in favor of bringing about in any way the social and political equality of the white and black races.' " Charles let Lincoln's words hang for a moment. "That crap came out of your mouth. Is that the same man who said 'All men are created equal?' "

"My personal wish is that all men everywhere be free," said Lincoln.

"That's nice. A little too apathetic for my taste. Let me ask you something. Did you believe we should have full political and social equality?"

"I wanted in all cases to do right. But I try not to be provoked by that to which I cannot properly offer an answer."

" 'No man knows better where the shoe pinches than the man who wears it.' "

"I said that." said Lincoln.

"You said a lot of things. At times you seemed to contradict yourself."

"I hold the value of life is to advance the condition of the honest, struggling laboring man."

"Bull!" Charles got up from his chair. "You just didn't know people would be digging up all your words all these years later. You'd have been more careful. Those words spoken in the heat of debate may have revealed more than you intended.

"Oh, I had to clean up after myself more than once in order, as I've said, to be elected. Else I would have been on the trash heap where a man lands at times for speaking his mind. All this nonsense about this or that man, this or that race, and one race being inferior, nonsense. Let's get on with it and come together as one people. No one has a right to enslave another. There is no justification. Stand up and unite for equality. This is the Declaration's principle."

"I think maybe you're a racist." Charles walked over to Lincoln and gave him a shove.

Lincoln sat forward, got up, and moved away.

"Don't back down. This is not the Blackhawk War you can just walk away from. Lock and load. Someone says you're a racist, that's cause for a duel. Or would you rather wrestle?" Charles crouched low with his arms held wide as he circled Lincoln. "You were a pretty good wrestler, right? Well, I lettered in high school in wrestling — all-state. A couple of opposing coaches wouldn't allow his white wrestlers to step on the mat with me."

"If I said something to rile you, I'm sorry," said Lincoln. "If I said something injurious to your character, I apologize." Lincoln knew from experience that it was a mistake to to be ruled by emotion, by rage, that he must conduct himself with cold, hard reason.

"This is plain old gut-level emotion, anger. You trying to walk away from a fight, Lincoln?"

"No, but this is foolish."

"Better than killing each other, wouldn't you say. You're face to face with the enemy." Charles eyed Lincoln, looking for chance to take him down. "What gets me is why it has taken a century and a half for you to get called on it. I suppose because those in power weren't offended. You got away with a lot of things because you made it sound good. Your words could sit up and beg. But face it, you're a racist."

"I am not a racist!" said Lincoln, adamantly.

"So why didn't you free the slaves sooner?"

"Because that would have been the end of constitutional government. I claim not to have controlled events, but confess plainly that events controlled me."

"That's convenient. You were a segregationist till the end."

"Charles," Lincoln took a moment to collect his thoughts. "Many people wanted rid of me. I had half-a-mind to let them have their way. At that point there was no more money. The bottom was out of the tub. I've always upheld your humanity and basic right to live your own life, but I was loathe to promise anything I could not deliver. I was unsure once the war ended that the freed slaves would not be forced back to the plantations. The 13th Amendment was a new birth of freedom, your freedom."

"You weren't cold in the grave before they tried passing new laws. The South was given the go-ahead by 1876 to treat the blacks any way they wanted, so we were back to square one."

"I gave my heart and soul to that Amendment."

"You can hammer out laws till you're blue in the face, but if people have no intention of obeying the law or enforcing the rule, it's tough sledding."

"But with the war won, it was time to move ahead. The 13th Amendment was a King's cure for all the evils," Lincoln insisted.

"We had another King's cure."

"The 13th Amendment was the promise of freedom. I made that promise. I tried to stay the course, keep my resolves, perhaps that's the chief gem of my character."

"This man was our leader," said Charles pointing to the photograph of Martin Luther King hanging on the wall. "He was assassinated trying to keep your promise. People were so mad they wanted to punch out every white face they saw. There were so many fires you couldn't see the Liberty statue atop the Capitol dome put there by those slaves you freed. I was back in hell, singing *We Shall Overcome* with gusto."

With that, Charles got the better of Lincoln, taking him down. "I was ready to be massacred like all the men, women, and children we were killing in Vietnam, but at least then I knew what I was fighting for." Charles was on top of Lincoln. "Same thing we'd always fought for. Justice, simple justice. Then when we got it, we discovered we couldn't eat it."

"I was afraid a race war would be the next civil war, but blood cannot restore blood," said Lincoln, looking up at Charles.

" 'Blood will flow in the streets of Birmingham before it'll be integrated.' Like a young man's blood, murdered, not for killing or stealing but for wearing a Congress of Racial Equality t-shirt. That young man was my big brother."

Charles struggled to keep Lincoln down. He managed to get him in a headlock. "His body was found in the Big Black River. There's been a lot of dead people who tried to claim the Declaration, tried to uphold you and your . . ."

". . . high-toned-holier-than-thou ideals," gasped Lincoln.

Charles found his hands around Lincoln's neck. Lincoln offered no resistance. Charles slowly released his hold. Lincoln stayed motionless for a moment before lifting himself up off the floor. They sat for a long time in silence. Lincoln was trying to comprehend what had transpired. He told Charles that he understood things had not worked out as he had wished and that his words had burdened those who tried to carry out their promise. He wished he had not said some things not because he didn't know they would come back to haunt him so many years later, but because they did his own true thoughts and feelings a disservice. He said it hurt him deeply that anyone would think he was not sympathetic to all aspects of the human condition. Admittedly, that his words had mattered at all was deeply gratifying. He thought the life, though, that Charles had endured was heart-wrenching.

"Charles, I am sorry about your father, and brother, and I'm sorry about your son."

"Yeah, I know." Charles stared straight ahead.

"I am," said Lincoln. "It may be of little comfort, but it has to be said. It must be said. I was wrong about certain things. I'm sorry."

Charles nodded. "You got my sympathy too, Lincoln. I know how it is to be poked, studied, labeled. I long ago tired of reading about the social state we were in. You're a consummate politician. You did what the situation demanded, did what we all do with life at times — we improvise. Things change though. I wanted to be as sure as I could about your mind, your words, your deeds, your heart."

"I should have done more. It was up to me how my life turned out," said Lincoln. "It was my responsibility. But in the end, man is an event which cannot judge itself, but for better or worse, is left to the judgment of others." Lincoln was determined to hold onto a cool logic but was absolutely adamant as he looked Charles square in the eye. "I'm only human, just like you. We all struggle as to how to conduct ourselves, what is honorable, and what is necessary for success. But if this country cannot be saved without giving up the principle of equality, I'd rather be assassinated on this spot than surrender to it."

Charles looked at Lincoln. Neither man blinked. Charles, at that moment, knew for the first time how committed Lincoln was. He believed him. Charles turned away, picking up the gun as he turned. With his back to Lincoln, he again quoted their favorite writer. " 'If it were done, when 'tis done, then 'twere well . . .' "

" 'It were done quickly.' *Macbeth*," answered Lincoln.

Charles walked to the window. The July Fourth celebrations were over; the streets were empty. America had survived to see another birthday and would probably live to see many more — if Lincoln's principles abided. Then Charles thought of his son, his innocence, his love. Charles wished his son could give him strength to go on, not to opt out. He looked at the gun in his hand, quoting, "If the assassination could trammel up the consequence, and catch with his surcease; that but this blow might be the be-all and end-all — here, but here, upon this bank and shoal of time, we'd jump the life to come."

Charles took a long pause and turned to Lincoln. "Did you ever think of suicide?"

"Came close to it a couple of times," said Lincoln.

"You had enough reasons," said Charles, "McClellan was running for president. Grant was bogged down. Sherman's supply lines were shredded. The newspapers were gloom and doom."

"And I thought marriage was to be my Waterloo. The decision of whether to marry or not 'bout drove me over the edge."

Lincoln took a step toward Charles. "Writing was a great outlet for my darker side.

> To ease me of this power to think,
> That through my bosom raves,
> I'll headlong leap from hell's high brink
> And wallow in its waves.

"I have been well acquainted with mental demons. I found from my trip as a young man down the Mississippi that the world could be a grim place, full of misery. Man's fate's an iffy proposition. My friends used to watch over me afraid I might do something foolish."

Charles was looking out the window at that moment and thought he could make out the Musician standing under a street lamp.

"A dear friend," Lincoln continued, "when she knew I was in one of my hangdog states would pay me a visit. 'I came to cheer you up, Abraham.' She would just appear at my door, and I was cheered. She was that pretty. Her eyes were as blue as the sky. We got along. But I was intimidated by her beauty. I didn't know how to talk to her. I was very shy around her. It was embarrassing. She often teased me. But our intimacy was such that words weren't really needed. I had learned to live alone with my thoughts. Then I loosened up and told her about my hopes and dreams. Of course my prospects were limited at best. She liked to read, too. We were very compatible in that way. We both took to books as a sort of refuge. We would take long walks. It seemed so natural that we were together. Her family owned a tavern and boardinghouse. I stayed there for a bit. They took pity on me and fed me a lot of good meals." Lincoln picked up a photo of Charles' wife, Darlene, and walked over to Charles at the window. The Musician was still visible.

"Ann was like your wife, she was that pretty."

Charles glanced at the photo of Darlene Lincoln was holding.

"If you know anything about my life, you know that fate reared its head. Ann took sick and never recovered, nor I'm afraid did I. It hit me hard, the finality of it all. I was the most miserable man living, didn't know if I'd ever be better. Figured I must die or be better." Lincoln then recited again from one of his favorite poems by William Knox.

Yea! Hope and despondency, pleasure and pain,
Are mingled together in sun-shine and rain;
And the smile and the tear, and the song and the dirge,
Still follow each other, like surge upon surge.
'Tis the wink of an eye, 'tis the draught of a breath,
From the blossoms of health, to the paleness of death.
From the gilded saloon, to the brier and the shroud
Oh, why should the spirit of mortal be proud!

"You keep reciting these maudlin poems," Charles said, "I'm going to shoot both of us!"

"I never dared carry a knife in my pocket until...." said Lincoln. "After my son's death my life seemed not to be worth living."

Lincoln hesitated and then spoke again:

And father cardinal, I have heard you say
that we shall see and know our friends in heaven
if that be true, we shall see our boys again.

Charles did not respond to the King John quote. Lincoln leaned his body so that his face was only inches from that of his tortured friend. "The death of a loved one is an awful burden to bear . . . especially if you try to bear it alone. Don't be afraid to open your misery for others to see. Suffering can be a badge of honor. Despair can be a door to greater depth and wisdom. You will discover a kind of enlightenment that will enable you to continue. There is, I know . . . "

"I don't like a man who knows and knows he knows," Charles interrupted.

"If I know anything," said Lincoln, "it is that peace of mind can be found when you turn your suffering into something positive. It takes work and patience and courage. It is a great struggle but you will endure, and your son's pride will shine. Your life can be a shrine to your boy."

"I'm not afraid to die," said Charles raising the gun so that it came between them.

"I know you're not. You have felt the heat of battle." Lincoln tried to think of a fitting joke or story that might lessen the somber mood, but for one of the rare times in his life, he was at a loss. He only knew the hard bottom of truth. "I think, based on my experience, I would avoid being idle. Stay busy and plod on. Sadder but wiser as they say."

Charles glanced out the window. The Musician was no longer under the street lamp. Strangely, Charles smiled and laid the gun on the sill. His eyes became moist. He sat down in the nearest chair, and the tears flowed freely.

"Do you dream about your boys?"

"I do," Lincoln said. "After our son Willie died, Mrs. Lincoln and I left the White House because it was too painful to remain, especially for Mary. We went to the Soldier's Home. The home had sheltered disabled and retired soldiers . . . "

"Didn't you hold a seance to try and communicate with your son?"

Lincoln hesitated before answering Charles' question.

"My wife did . . . she was extremely despondent . . . . I reckon if folks knew that I was susceptible to periods of such doubt and behavior . . . at times I seemed to have my own little grey cloud over my head. If they had been aware of such things and then surmised that I would end up freeing the slaves . . . well, I never would have made it out of Illinois." Charles realized Lincoln was attempting some light-heartedness out of concern for him.

"I dream about my boy, my Richie. I miss him. God, I miss him," said Charles.

"You may my glories and my state depose, But not my griefs, still I am king of those."

"*Richard the Second*," said Charles without missing a beat.

TWENTY - SEVEN

"When my boy was young, I read to him from a children's book of Shakespeare. I had him reading all the plays. I told him he could find whatever he needed in Shakespeare."

"But it is children who give us courage," Lincoln remarked.

Charles considered that thought for a moment. He looked at the closed door to his son's room, his thoughts going back two years earlier when he gave Richie one of his most prized possessions — the little book of Shakespeare that his teacher had give him before he went to Vietnam. "Come in," had come the reply to Charles' knock. He had opened his son's bedroom door to see Richie putting on the coat of his Marine dress blues. It was the first time Charles had seen his son in uniform. Richie finished buttoning the coat up and turned to his father. "How do I look?"

Charles could find no words — finally he murmured, "Like a hero." He started to leave, but turned back. "Richie, just don't try to be John Wayne."

"Who's John Wayne?"

Charles was speechless. Suddenly he started laughing.

"What's so funny?" Richie wanted to know.

Charles looked at his son and simply shrugged his shoulders. "I love you, " he said and then hugged Richie tightly. It was sort of an awkward, but memorable, bear hug. "Oh, I almost forgot — thought you might want this," Charles said, holding out the little book of Shakespeare.

Richie took the book. It was unfamiliar to him. Charles had kept it in storage with a few other items from *his* war.

"It looks used," Richie said.

In the kitchen the television was on low in the background. CNN was doing a retrospective on the war and at that moment was commenting on President Bush's dramatic landing by fighter jet on the deck of the aircraft carrier, *Abe Lincoln,* to announce victory over Iraq. There was a cake decorated with candles and a sparkler in the middle of the table. Charles sat down at the table. Darlene sat across from him.

"Another sucker," Charles said. "I had no business being there, and he has no business going to Iraq. 'Who's John Wayne?' I didn't know whether to laugh or cry. Seeing that uniform . . . it wasn't real before."

"I was so in love. You were so sexy in that uniform."

At that moment, Richie appeared in his uniform with the book of Shakespeare in hand. "I got more of this down to memory than you," Richie said waving the book in his hand.

"I doubt that," said Charles, trying to hide his emotion. Son and father had long been having spirited competitions as to who could identify a certain quote from one of Shakespeare's plays. Winning the game was how Richie could win his father's approval for something he wanted to do — like borrowing the car. Richie saw the birthday cake. Darlene lit the candles and sparkler, and she and Charles sang "Happy birthday to you . . ."

When Richie was little, his parents had told him all the fireworks were for his birthday. He thought it was special that his birthday was on July Fourth. After the song, Darlene cut the cake, and all had a second helping accompanied by the grace of family laughter. Finally Richie excused himself, telling his parents, "Charlotte's waiting for me."

"Is that why you're wearing your uniform?" Darlene asked.

"She thinks it's hot," Richie mumbled, embarrassed. "I gotta go. We're gonna be late for the fireworks."

"Your father was very hot in his uniform, too."

Charles ignored his wife's compliment and challenged Richie with a Shakespeare quote:

> What's in a name? That which we call a rose
> By any other name would smell as sweet.

Richie laughed. "Easy. Capulet: *Romeo and Juliet*."

Charles allowed that he had given his son an easy one, but if he was not home before midnight, it would be no holds barred.

"It's my birthday, and there's a dance," Richie looked to his mother for reinforcement.

"You a dancer?" Charles teased.

"Yeah," Richie shrugged to his father's question. "You know I like to dance."

"Your father had some moves," said Darlene.

Richie laughed.

Charles frowned. "What's so funny?"

Richie smiled. "Show me."

Charles shook his head, looking at Darlene. "Your son is challenging me. 'Show me,' " he muttered.

"Show me, too," Darlene urged.

Charles nodded his head and eased his body up from the chair. He gave a little hitch to his pants and showed a few moves that would have made Michael Jackson proud.

Richie and Darlene voiced their approval.

"Now you show me what *you* got. A real dancer has to strut his stuff."

Richie slowly removed the jacket of his uniform, and then turned the kitchen into his stage where he brought down the house with his moves, receiving a standing ovation from his mother.

For a moment, Charles remained stonefaced, and then broke into a big smile. "All right, but I don't care how sweet little Charlotte smells, Romeo, 1:00 A.M."

Richie headed for the door.

"Not so fast, soldier. Tell your mother good night."

"Give the boy some peace," said Darlene.

"That's all I do. He takes one piece after another."

"Get on out of here," Darlene told her son, draping her arm around Charles' shoulder. "I got business with your father."

"Love you," said Richie, hurrying out the door.

"I should hope so," was the quick good-natured reply from Charles to the closed door.

"Well, soldier boy, just you and me now."

"Guess there's going to be an adjustment. You want to read a book?"

"Don't make me get violent."

◆　◆　◆

Charles and Lincoln stood in Richie's room. Charles had not been able to step into his son's room since the road-side bomb took Richie's life in Iraq. Not a thing had been touched. One wall was decorated with a few photographs of Charles' ancestors that Richie had collected. They had been among the possessions of Charles' father in an old shoe box he'd left behind when he left for good. Richie had arranged a family tree. He had charted Charles's family back before they arrived in America.

"His hobby was . . . finding out about his ancestors, genealogy. Richie found out his great-great-great grandfather was a runaway slave from Georgia." The boy's passion for his subject always brought a smile to Charles' face, though Charles had never been too enthused about looking back for his family's history. He hadn't thought tracing his family's origins was possible, but he said nothing to discourage Richie.

Richie's enthusiasm for his research was such that Charles had become immersed in it. He also wanted to know as much as possible about their ancestors. It was more than he could have ever wished for. Richie discovered that his great-great grandfather had escaped to Missouri — a free state — then was kidnapped and taken back to Georgia. A slave owner could seize and recapture his slave wherever he could.

Lincoln reminded Charles, "the slave owner was judge and jury. Every free person of color was vulnerable to arrest and worse."

"According to Richie's research," Charles told Lincoln, "Richie's great-great-great grandfather manged to escape again, and ended up back in Missouri where he filed a lawsuit to remain free."

Darlene had joked that she had nothing so exciting in her background other than that some of her ancestors had apparently been in debtors' prison in England and had been given the choice of

Australia or America.

Charles had told Richie, "I rescued your mother. She married *up* in life."

Charles laughed again at the memory.

Lincoln saw a picture sitting on the dresser. It was of Charles, Darlene, and Richie from Richie's high school graduation. Richie's acceptance letter to Princeton was tacked to a bulletin board.

"Princeton?"

"Surprised?"

"Impressed," Lincoln said, nodding his head, admittedly a little surprised, considering what he remembered about Princeton.

"Richie had been upset that some classmates said he had an advantage 'cause he was black and that's why he got accepted. He had the grades. He studied hard. Do a few kids getting a helping hand into school 'cause they're black make up for all the years of misery and suffering? How many yoyos get into Yale every year 'cause their daddy, their grandaddy, and their great-grandaddy all went to school there? Legacy admissions are affirmative action for dumb white kids. You had a boy go to Harvard, didn't you?"

"Yes," Lincoln nodded.

"He got in on his merit alone?"

"I'd like to think so."

"Maybe he did, but I don't think the fact that he was the President's son hurt him any, do you?"

"I imagine that it did not harm his chances. Though," Lincoln smiled, "though if he had wished to attend the University of South Carolina he might have been sorely disappointed."

"Did you send him money?"

"Yes," said Lincoln a little puzzled.

"No one asked him where he got it?"

"Why would they?"

"Exactly." Charles said. "Your boy was a good student?"

"Yes, pretty much so."

"But he didn't have 'credit to my race' stamped on his forehead?"

"No," Lincoln said knowingly.

"Were people afraid of him?"

"No."

"So," Charles said, "I don't want to hear anymore about equal chance."

The questions Charles asked Lincoln were questions Charles knew his son had not wanted to be confronted with.

"A black man can't just be good? He's got to be great! I tutored my boy every night. I put too much pressure on him, pushed him too fast. He wasn't ready. Maybe he thought it wasn't possible for him to be what I wanted. He was a fine young man. Smart. You ever want to be black?"

Lincoln was silent as he considered Charles' question.

"You feel sorry for me?"

"Do I seem so vulgar? A long time ago," Lincoln said, "I knew a man, old man. His job was to clean and empty outhouses. An ex-slave, his name was White. Lived on Blue Road in Greentown. Ear had been cut off, to mark him, I guess. His back was one big scar from flogging, mounds of skin left to heal any old way. Every time I saw him, I thanked God I was white."

"Pain and shame," Charles said, shaking his head. "That old man. He's in your face, can't miss it. Can't help but hate it. But it goes deeper than that, Lincoln. Racism's in the pores, like a virus, and some people, good people, don't know they got it. Or they just accept it. They see Michael Jordan, Tiger Woods, Colin Powell . . .

they think everything's hunky-dory. Daddy said, when a white man said hello to him, he thought he'd made his day. I feel that sometimes. We're used to it."

"Don't get used to it," Lincoln said firmly. "Like the man said about skinning eels; 'It doesn't hurt them so very much. It's been going on for a long time, they're used to it.' "

"I see that old man, inferiority stamped on his face. Some mornings shaving I look in the mirror, see him looking back at me."

"What did he see?"

"Somebody who'd break in his house and knock him over the head."

"We must stop knocking each other over the head . . .. Charles, repeal the Declaration, repeal all past history, but you can't repeal human nature. It'll still be the abundance of man's heart, that racism is wrong; and out of the abundance of his heart, his mouth will continue to speak."

"Who's listening?"

"The better angels of our nature."

"The 'better angels' are doing us in while we stand around pretending not to know better so people like you'll feel responsible."

TWENTY - EIGHT

Charles and Lincoln stood across the street, out of view from a nice little one-story carriage house. It was Charles' mother-in-law's house where Darlene had moved six months before. Her parents had some years ago moved out of the suburbs into the D.C. district. It was the reverse of what many people were doing at the time, but a grandson was the draw.

"Knock on the door," said Lincoln. Charles gave Lincoln a look. "You're a brave man. You can do it." Charles considered doing as Lincoln suggested, but turned away.

They soon found themselves back at the Lincoln Memorial. It was well after midnight, and there was no one about aside from a couple of armed security officers. Charles walked up and sat on the Memorial steps. Lincoln sat down on the steps and took a letter out of his hat. He carefully unfolded it and read aloud the letter.

"I pray that our heavenly Father will assuage the anguish of your bereavement, and leave you only the cherished memory of the loved and lost, and the solemn pride that is yours, to have laid so costly a sacrifice upon the altar of freedom."

Lincoln looked at Charles. "I am not a very sentimental man, but may this sentiment be yours."

"I wish that it could be," Charles said in dismay.

Lincoln upended his hat, newspaper clippings fell to the ground. Charles looked among the fallen items.

"These are all rave reviews, Lincoln." He spotted a confederate five-dollar bill and asked Lincoln about it.

"Insurance," Lincoln, joked. He crumpled the letter he had read aloud and gathered the clippings that had fallen out of his hat and threw them in the trash. "The letter's a sham just like all these newspaper clippings."

He walked up into the Memorial and walked to where the second inaugural speech was engraved.

"I was so relieved when the war was over. I felt redeemed, relieved, off the hook. I was looking forward to a second term. It was a great honor. Would've been a great labor. I did all I could for the good of mankind."

"Makes you feel good?"

"When I do good, I feel good," Lincoln replied. "When I do bad, I feel bad. That's my religion."

"What is this goodness kick?"

"The white man's burden. Emancipation fell short, I know. Like the lawyer who tried to establish a calf had five legs by calling the tail a leg. Proclaiming slaves free didn't make them free. They were still far removed from being placed on an equality with the white race. I'm in the dumps, almost ready to hang myself."

Charles started walking away.

"Where you going?"

"I've got some rope stored back here," Charles said, grinning, continuing off into the wing of the Memorial.

Lincoln looked up at the words of his second inaugural. He read aloud hoping to see if the words were as wise as he thought they might be when he wrote them.

"Fondly do we hope, fervently do we pray that this mighty scourge of war may speedily pass away. Yet, if God wills that it continue, until all the wealth piled by the bondman's two hundred and fifty years of unrequited toil shall be sunk . . . ."

Charles returned and joined Lincoln, not looking at the engraved words, but speaking from memory.

". . . and until every drop of blood drawn with the lash, shall be paid by another drawn with the sword, as was said three thousand years ago, so still it must be said 'the judgments of the Lord, are true and righteous altogether.' " Charles then tossed the rope noose to Lincoln.

"Nigger necktie. Found it in your lap."

"Emancipation did not unmake prejudice, I'm sad to say." Lincoln put the rope aside.

"And no people were ever less prepared for freedom," said Charles. He looked up at Lincoln's words again and spoke them out loud as he had done so many times before.

Charles, like Lincoln, was trying to reconsider those words, to determine if they were as meaningful as he once thought they were:

The dogmas of the quiet past are inadequate to the stormy past. The fiery trial through which we pass, will light us down, in honor or dishonor, to the latest generation. The occasion's piled high with difficulty. We must rise with the occasion. With malice toward none; with charity for all; with firmness in the right, as God gives us to see the right, let's strive on to finish the work we're in; to bind up the nation's wounds; to care for him who's borne the battle, and for his widow, and for his orphan, to do all which may achieve a just, and lasting peace, among ourselves, and with all . . . ."

"I'm sorry."

"I hear you. I'm sorry too," said Charles. "But my son just wanted to get on with it. People don't want to hear your words; they just want to pay a lot of money for them."

Charles turned to look at the wall where the Gettysburg Address was inscribed. There was nothing there. He walked up to the wall and touched the smooth marble. The wall was blank. He turned around. Lincoln was gone. Charles ran down the steps. The Musician was sitting on the other side. Charles saw the cart sitting nearby. The cardboard sign reading "Keep to the rhythm and you won't get lost" caught his eye. He walked past the cart and along the path leading to the Vietnam Memorial Wall.

A few people were still paying their respects. Charles watched as a young Asian woman set a candle in front of the wall. An Asian man, close in age, stood behind her holding the hand of a girl in her teens. Charles assumed the girl was their daughter. The woman held out her hand to the girl, pointing to one of the engraved names. She ran the girl's hands over the lettering. Then the woman lit a match and helped the girl light the candle. Charles saw the woman take something from around her neck and set it by the candle. She took the hands of her husband and daughter, as they walked off into the night.

Charles watched them go. He walked over where the woman had been standing by the wall. He knelt down by the candle. Next to it was a chain with a small statue of the Virgin Mary. He looked at the names above the candle, and there he saw "William Hutton." Charles looked around for the family, but they were gone. He rose up and hurriedly tried to see if he could spot them, but there was only the Musician sitting nearby in his multi-colored fatigues. He took out a harmonica and started to play.

◆　◆　◆

Charles found himself in front of the National Museum of American History where he and Darlene had gone with Richie to see his ancestor's documents that had been filed in the fight for freedom before Lincoln's war. It had been so uplifting for both son and father to discover that their ancestor did not beg for freedom but demanded it in a way that was both courageous and desperate.

We owe it to the fallen, he thought, to keep going, keep pushing the rock up the hill, keep trying, as Lincoln would say, to do for those who cannot do for themselves. They too had lost loved ones, lost entire families, lost their names, lost their histories. This was what Richie was trying to resurrect for his family.

◆　◆　◆

Charles found a seat at a small nearby cafe away from a couple of gentlemen enjoying their cigars. He turned to see Lincoln sitting at a table in a corner. There was no movement from Lincoln, who was obviously morose. His eyes stared down at the table. He did not seem to notice Charles approaching. There were a couple of empty beer bottles on the table. Surely they could not be Lincoln's, Charles thought, knowing Lincoln was known to drink very little.

"What do I owe you?" asked Lincoln, without raising his head.

"Forty acres and a Lexus," deadpanned Charles. Lincoln was puzzled.

"It's a joke," said Charles.

"I don't like to be diddled." Lincoln looked up. "Oh, it's you, Charles. Won't you join me?" Charles took a seat. There was a long silence. "At the very least," Lincoln finally said, "I was pandering to racism, which is even worse."

Charles looked at Lincoln, understanding that this could not be an easy admission for him. "So bad that it can drive a man to drink?"

Lincoln moved out of his forelorned position and picked up a bottle of beer. "There has been a proneness for the brilliant and warm blooded to fall into this vice . . .," Lincoln noted. "Leaves me flabby and undone. If I was to have a drink and cigar, you're the man I would like to have them with."

"I thought I read somewhere that you sold whiskey in a tavern?"

"Briefly," said Lincoln still holding the bottle.

"You're pretty handy with a beer bottle, Lincoln. You seem like you've handled a few before."

"Many a bottle passed through my hands to other hands. But if there is anything which it is the duty of the whole people to never entrust to any hands but their own, that thing is the preservation and perpetuity of their own liberties, and institutions."

"You just can't help yourself, can you?"

"A man who has no vices has damned few virtues," said Lincoln. "Besides drinkers' heads and hearts are good, better than most. So too their stories."

"The more you drink the better the story?"

"Probably the case. Never underestimate the value of embellishment."

Lincoln held out his left hand,

"What if this cursed hand
were thicker than itself with Brother's blood . . ."

Charles knew the King's speech from *Hamlet,* well,

"Is there not rain enough
in the Sweet heavens
To wash it white as snow?

"I thought about this speech often, especially when the war was
at its grimmest,

My fault is past, but, O, what form of prayer
Can forgive my turn? Forgive my foul murder.

Charles continued as did Lincoln's lament,

That cannot be . . .

Lincoln nodded, continuing,

For I still possess the effects for
Which I did the murder.
What then? What rests?

Charles shrugged,

Try what repentance can, what can it not?

Lincoln's face fell in despair,

"Yet what can it, when one can not Repent?"

Charles commiserated with Lincoln as they quickly traded quotes.

"O wretched state! O bosom black as death!"

"O limed soul, that struggling to be Free Art more engaged!"

"Help, angels!"

"Make assay."

"Bow, stubborn knee; and Heart with strings of steel . . . ."

Lincoln slipped from his chair and literally obeyed Charles' quote from Shakespeare, going down on his knees as though to pray. Charles joined him as Lincoln said . . . "Be soft as sinews of the newborn Babe."

Then together, Charles and Lincoln spoke the words . . . "All may be well."

Charles looked at Lincoln and said, "And if it's not, we'll just have to make the best of it. So there's no use crying in your beer now."

They got to their feet and walked out of the cafe. Once outside, they heard the Musician again weaving his music magic with the spiritual *Over My Head*. The music carried them along. Lincoln was concerned that people would not believe him to be a man of peace.

"Our continued turmoil's punishment for our sins. Damn! I'm ashamed. It should not have been this difficult. The more a man speaks, the less he is understood. The problem is in using the word "liberty." We do not all mean the same thing. The shepherd drives the wolf from the sheep's throat, for which the sheep thanks the shepherd as a liberator, while the wolf denounces him for the same act as the destroyer of liberty, especially as the sheep was a black one. There's bad faith somewhere. A golden opportunity was lost. We've not trusted one another. This disappoints me bitterly."

"I'm not dancing," said Charles.

"Defeat and failure in the field make everything seem wrong."

"Nothing is wrong," said Charles, hesitatingly.

"Except nothing is wrong," finished Lincoln. Then he started laughing.

Charles joined him, laughing long and hard.

They walked on in silence for awhile. Charles finally said something about his tank running on empty, but, he added, "it's full on frustration. 'Used to feel a part of something, I think. Maybe I was just fooling myself. I never felt more on my own than when I returned from Vietnam. I wonder if when my great-great-grandfather won his freedom, he danced? Or did he still feel alone in this country. As a people, I guess we've always felt alone because we were. My son felt that, I think."

"If destruction be our lot, we must ourselves be its author and finisher. As a nation of free men, we must live through all time, or die by suicide.

"Right now it's pretty much of a toss-up."

"But we," Lincoln said, "you and I hold the power, and bear the responsibility."

"Oh no, this is your party, the fireworks are all yours."

"If we don't accept the call, we might as well be on another planet."

Lincoln carried on with his argument, holding that their case was new, so they had to think anew, and act anew.

"Well, I can't be sold anymore, but I could be bought."

"We're being challenged. The fiery trial through which we pass, will light us down, in honor or dishonor, to the latest generation. We know how to save the Union."

"Is it worth saving?"

"We shall nobly save, or meanly lose, the last best, hope of earth. The way is plain, peaceful, generous, just — a way which, if followed, the world will forever applaud, and God must forever bless."

"Sounds like a fairy tale," said Charles.

"It will be and the emancipation will be waste paper, unless you watch it every day, and hour, and force it. Till all racists, like tallow-candles, flicker in the socket, die out, stink in the dark for a brief season, and be remembered no more, even by the smell."

Charles shook his head saying he had other things to think about. Lincoln said the struggle was a people's contest and Charles had to find a way to re-engage himself.

"If people didn't listen to you, why would they listen to me?"

Lincoln reminded Charles what he had said about people being willing to buy his words but not really listen to them. "You can reason with them," persuaded Lincoln.

"I have no more reasons."

"Then what is the choice? Don't be like the man on the boat who touches neither sail nor pump, but is merely a passenger, a deadhead at that, who expects to be carried snug and dry, throughout the storm, and safely landed right side up. Every edge must be made to cut. To win a war . . . ."

Lincoln paused, waiting for Charles to finish the sentence.

Charles did . . . "you have to fight."

"Yes," Lincoln said, "because how hard it is to die and leave one's country no better than if one had never lived for it." Charles stopped walking. Lincoln sensed the emotion. He put his arm around Charles.

"I want the whole mess to be gone, over," consoled Lincoln.

"When I'm president that's when it'll be over."

"You got my vote," Lincoln assured him.

"You did good. We've come a long way. You did the right thing."

"Don't spare me," insisted Lincoln.

"You know me better by now," laughed Charles.

"There are no excuses for some of the things I said. Just a vote-hungry politician."

"You got rid of a vile institution. You took a great chance. Without you there'd be no country, no July Fourth to celebrate."

"An idea that I came up short on . . . a difficult issue."

"Without you, nobody'd care about promises, broken or other-wise."

Lincoln valued Charles' opinion and was pleased to know, in Charles' judgement "the little I did or said was not entirely a failure. None of us are off the hook. We have all done wrong. Even Jefferson." Lincoln considered what he'd just said. "It's not about blame or guilt."

"What's it about?"

"Privilege," said Lincoln.

TWENTY - NINE

They stood in front of the New York Avenue Presbyterian church where a special midnight freedom service was underway. Lincoln had visited the original church building once in a while because the preacher didn't preach politics. Lights shone through the beautiful stained glass windows of the new church. The gospel song *Were You There* could be heard. Charles had not been to church since his son was killed. He had found no help in the church. Who was watching over his son? The Lord had fallen down on the job. "He could not prevent harm coming to my son," Charles told Darlene. With all the death and devastation, how could God be here? Charles asked himself.

Charles and Lincoln walked up the stairs and through the big oak doors of the massive church. There was something about a building of such scale and beauty that quieted the soul if only temporarily. Lincoln walked in behind Charles, and they sat at the back of the congregation.

◆ ◆ ◆

"I never joined a congregation. A politician has to be careful not to offend," said Lincoln adjusting his knees in the tight pew.

"You know the Bible?"

"It's got some good quotes. I was at a religious service," whispered Lincoln, "preacher asked everyone to stand who wanted to go to Heaven. Lot of people got up. Then he asked all who didn't want to go to hell to stand. Everybody else got up but me. Preacher said, 'Mr. Lincoln, where you going?' I told him I was going to Congress. I'm not much of a judge of religion, but if I get to Heaven, I hope it's more pleasing than Congress."

Charles noticed the church was three-quarters full of people, many African-Americans. A choir was singing. Lincoln recalled thousands on the White House lawn singing. He told Charles that he had wanted to join them.

"Nobody stopping you now," said Charles. At that moment a young choir member, stepped forward from the choir and performed a spirited hip-hop, rap rendition of the Gettysburg Address amid congregational clapping and shouts of "Amen." Lincoln was enraptured. He leaned forward in the pew listening intently as the young choir member strutted his stuff accompanied by a sax man, drummer and piano player.

> Four score and seven years ago our fathers brought forth
> on this continent a new nation, conceived in liberty, and ded-
> icated to the proposition that all men are created equal.

The church goers were delighted. Lincoln wasn't sure if the response was to the words or to the young choir member's talent.

He decided that it didn't matter. The people were having a good time.

> Now we are engaged in a great civil war, testing
> whether that nation, or any nation, so conceived and so
> dedicated, can long endure.

There were more shouts of "Amen" from the congregation.

> We are met on a great battle-field of that war.
> We have come to dedicate a portion of that field, as a
> final resting place for those who here gave their lives that
> that nation might live. It is altogether fitting and proper
> that we should do this.

The young choir member was now speaking faster, his emotion seemed raw, coming from a deep place.

> But, in a larger sense, we can not dedicate — we can
> not consecrate — we can not hallow — this ground. The
> brave men, living and dead, who struggled here, have con-
> secrated it, far above our poor power to add or detract.
> The world will little note, nor long remember what we
> say here, but it can never forget what they did here. It is
> for us the living, rather, to be dedicated here to the unfin-
> ished work which they who fought here have thus far so
> nobly advanced.

Some members of the congregation stood up and continued clapping. Charles stood too, and Lincoln joined him.

It is rather for us to be here dedicated to the great task remaining before us — that from these honored dead we take increased devotion to that cause for which they gave the last full measure of devotion — that we here highly resolve that these dead shall not have died in vain — that this nation, under God . . .

The shouts of "Amen" were loud. There were shouts of "Yes, Lord" as all the people were now standing and clapping in a great chorus of one.

shall have a new birth of freedom — and that govern- ment of the people, by the people, for the people shall not perish from the earth.

The choir and congregation erupted in cheers and applause as did Charles and Lincoln. Charles looked at Lincoln and saw tears in his eyes.

"You're right. Children give us courage," said Charles closing his eyes, realizing this was the first time he had felt any sense of joy since losing his son.

"What did you see in that young man's face?" asked Lincoln as they made their way back to the Memorial.

"Hope," answered Charles. "Black folks are nothing if not hopeful. Have always been, will always be."

THIRTY

Charles and Lincoln stood on the Mall looking toward the Memorial. Lincoln almost forgot he was wearing the 'Air Jordan' shoes.

"These have felt real good on my feet, so good that I could challenge you to a race."

Charles thought about Lincoln's offing. "How about a dash to the Memorial steps?"

"You're on," said Lincoln. "Call it."

"On you mark, get set, go!"

It was no race. Charles won going away.

"You should know that the hundred yard dash is the black man's domain."

Lincoln laughed. "Used to be able to outrun my fellow lawyers in my boots."

"We had plenty of practice, running away from the slave owners." Charles thought for a moment, remembering, at his age, how easy and good it felt to run. Maybe slavery's curse clung to him just as easily.

The Musician was playing an up-tempo version of "This Little Light of Mine" on the sax.

"Never played a musical instrument, can't sing, can't dance," said Lincoln shaking his head. "But I know good music when I hear it." He swayed to the music, his coat fluttering around him, causing him to look like a thin locust tree waving in the wind.

"You gotta let yourself go," said Charles. "Like this," performing a little step.

Lincoln laughed. "I'll leave the movement to you."

"Come on, you got your dancing shoes on."

"They didn't help me out in our little race."

The Musician continued playing.

"Sway a little, move your hips. Like this." Again Charles showed Lincoln what he meant. "Let the spirit move you."

Lincoln tried.

"That's it! Now pat your feet."

Lincoln followed Charles' lead.

"Now wave your hands."

Lincoln followed suit.

"Now let's clap. Keep your feet going. Keep clapping. You're gettin' it . . ."

Lincoln did get it.

Charles sang, "This light of mine, I'm gonna let it shine . . . Come on Lincoln, I'm not singin' solo." They sang and danced. "The body's enlightened."

"So's the mind," said Lincoln.

"You got rhythm, Abraham."

"As do you, Charles, as do you."

Lincoln stopped dancing. He laughed and retrieved his hat. Neither spoke. It was an awkward moment for both.

"Well," said Lincoln, "This is about enough fun for one night." At the top of the Memorial steps, he sat down and proceeded to take the Air Jordans off and put on his boots.

As the lawyer said, "I had no business here, but . . ." Charles finished Lincoln's sentence.

" 'I had none anywhere else.' You told me that one."

"Did I tell you the time I was at the opera and laid my hat on the seat beside me? This portly woman came along and sat down right on it. I said, 'Madam I could've told you my hat wouldn't fit before you tried it on.' "

Charles grinned. Lincoln picked something up off the floor. It was a penny.

"Finding a penny's supposed to be good luck. Take a look at it."

Lincoln did and raised an eyebrow. He looked at Charles.

"Yep. That's you. Penny's my kind of coin. Real common. Guess that's why you're on it."

"Common-looking people are the best in the world. That's why the Lord made so many of them. Being a superstitious fellow, I'll give this to you to hold onto." Lincoln flipped the penny to Charles.

Charles looked at the coin for a second. "Some people want to get rid of the penny. Say it's not relevant, worthless. A penny for your thoughts."

"There were some," Lincoln said, "who felt that was about all my thoughts were worth. It always comes down to the same thing," said Lincoln. "A people's government for a people's good. I distrust the wisdom, if not the sincerity of friends, who hold my hands while my enemies stab me. Beware of surrendering a political power which you already possess, and which, if surrendered, will surely be used to close the door of advancement against you. When you're President, just do the best you know how and hope it brings you out right. And remember, public opinion's everything in this country."

The sun's first orange rays appearing on the horizon found Charles sitting on the same park bench he had been on when Lincoln first appeared, the tabloid paper with Lincoln's picture as a woman beside him. Charles glanced at it. A soft clip-clop of horses' hooves echoed down the path. Charles heard a bell ringing. He looked up to see the Musician pushing his cart away whistling *The Battle Hymn of the Republic*.

Charles got up from the bench and walked over to the reflecting pool. He splashed a little water on his face. He then walked up the steps of Lincoln's Memorial.

Park employees milled about getting ready for the day. Charles looked up at the statue of Lincoln. He walked around the statue and looked up at the wall. The words of the Gettysburg Address were back where they belonged.

Inside the gift shop, Charles poured coffee into his mug and took a sip. Then he put a double sugar in and stirred. He sampled the coffee again — it had not improved. Back outside Charles removed the rope barrier. A handful of tourists ambled in. Another day. Then Charles did a double-take. There, sitting on the top step of the Memorial was a pair of Air Jordan shoes.

◆ ◆ ◆

Charles, dressed in a suit, stood on the sidewalk in front of his mother-in-law's house. He climbed the steps and rang the doorbell. A moment later Darlene opened the door. They both stood there for a moment. Darlene reached out and touched Charles' face. He took her hand. Tears welled in her eyes and she smiled, a smile Charles had missed. He reached out and pulled her gently to him.

The next morning's sun glowed as Charles and Darlene knelt before their son's gravestone. The Musician was alone on the steps of the Lincoln Memorial. He was finishing lacing up the pair of Air Jordans. He put on his sunglasses and put the sax to his lips and played *Amazing Grace*. The sun bathed the Mall, the Washington Monument, the Capitol, and the statue atop the Capitol dome, Liberty in pure light.

OTHER BOOKS by the AUTHOR

In and Out of the Shadows
(a book of photos and poems)

My Mother's Autumn
(a book of poems)

Happenstance
(a book of poems)

A Better Place
(memoir and social commentary of the
author's home state of West Virginia)

PLAYS by the AUTHOR

Where's Nova Scotia

Final Assault

Lincoln and James

ABOUT THE AUTHOR

David Selby is an actor and writer.
He lives in California with his wife and family.